ALSO BY PETER CAMERON

One Way or Another
Leap Year
Far-flung
The Weekend
Andorra
The Half You Don't Know
The City of Your Final Destination

SOMEDAY THIS PAIN WILL BE USEFUL TO YOU

PETER CAMERON

someday
this
pain
will
be
useful
to
you

FRANCES FOSTER BOOKS
FARRAR, STRAUS AND GIROUX
NEW YORK

A portion of this novel originally appeared on nerve.com

*The author wishes to express his gratitude to Anoukh Foerg,
Frances Foster, Michael Martin, Irene Skolnick, the John
Simon Guggenheim Memorial Foundation, the MacDowell
Colony, and the Corporation of Yaddo.*

Copyright © 2007 by Peter Cameron
All rights reserved
Distributed in Canada by Douglas & McIntyre Ltd.
Printed in the United States of America
Designed by Jay Colvin
First edition, 2007
3 5 7 9 10 8 6 4

www.fsgkidsbooks.com

Library of Congress Cataloging-in-Publication Data
Cameron, Peter, date.
    Someday this pain will be useful to you / Peter Cameron.— 1st ed.
        p. cm.
    Summary: Eighteen-year-old James living in New York City with
his older sister and divorced mother struggles to find a direction for
his life.
    ISBN-13: 978-0-374-30989-3
    ISBN-10: 0-374-30989-2
    1. Conduct of life—Fiction.   2. Interpersonal relations—Fiction.
3. Self-perception—Fiction.   4. New York (N.Y.)—Fiction.]   I. Title.

PZ7.C14347 Som 2007
[Fic]—dc22

2006043747

For Justin Richardson
and in memory of
Marie Nash Shaw
1900–1993

Be patient and tough; someday this pain
will be useful to you.
—Ovid

When you long with all your heart for someone to love
you, a madness grows there that shakes all sense from the
trees and the water and the earth. And nothing lives for
you, except the long deep bitter want. And this is what
everyone feels from birth to death.
—Denton Welch
Journal, 8 May 1944, 11.15 p.m.

SOMEDAY THIS PAIN WILL BE USEFUL TO YOU

Thursday, July 24, 2003

THE DAY MY SISTER, GILLIAN, DECIDED TO PRONOUNCE her name with a hard G was, coincidentally, the same day my mother returned, early and alone, from her honeymoon. Neither of these things surprised me. Gillian, who was between her third and fourth years at Barnard, was dating a "language theory" professor named Rainer Maria Schultz and had consequently become a bit of a linguistic zealot, often ranting about something called "pure" language, of which Gillian with a hard G was supposedly an example. My mother, on the other hand, had rather rashly decided to marry an odd man named Barry Rogers. Gillian—Gillian—and I had both suspected that this marriage (my mother's third) would not last very long, but we assumed it would survive its honeymoon, although when we heard they were planning a honeymoon in Las Vegas our skepticism grew. My mother, who has spent her entire life avoiding places like Las

Vegas and merrily disdaining anyone who visited, or even con-
templated visiting, such places, had announced, in a disturbing
brainwashy way, that a honeymoon in Las Vegas would be "fun"
and a nice change from her previous honeymoons (Italy with my
father and the Galápagos Islands with her second husband).
Whenever my mother said anything was, or would be, "fun" you
could take it as a warning that said thing was not nor would be at
all fun, and when I reminded my mother of this—I used the example of her telling me that the sailing camp she had forced me to
attend the summer I was twelve would be "fun"—she admitted
that sailing camp had not been fun for me but that was no reason
why a honeymoon in Las Vegas would not be fun for her. Such is
the ability adults—well, my mother, at least—have to deceive
themselves.

Gillian and I were eating lunch, or some midday meal approx-
imate to lunch, when my mother untimely returned from her honeymoon. It was about two o'clock in the afternoon. Gillian sat at
the kitchen table doing the *New York Times* crossword, which we
were not allowed to do when my mother was home because, as she
often told us, it was the only dependable pleasure in her life. I was
eating a fried egg sandwich. I was supposed to have been working
at the art gallery which my mother owned but which was effec-
tively run by a young man named John Webster, but John had
sensibly decided that since my mother was safely out of town,
preoccupied with whatever unthinkable activities preoccupy a
fifty-three-year-old woman in Las Vegas on her third honeymoon,
and since it was July, and no one had set foot in the gallery for several days, he would close the gallery and go and stay with friends

in Amagansett, and I could do whatever I wanted for the rest of the week. I was not, of course, to tell my mother about this hiatus, for she believed that at any moment someone might walk in off the street and buy a garbage can decoupaged with pages torn out of varied editions of the Bible, the Torah, or the Koran (for $16,000). My mother opened the gallery about two years ago after she divorced her second husband, because she wanted to "do" something, which you might have thought meant work, but did not: "doing" something entailed buying a lot of new clothes (very expensive clothes that had been "deconstructed," which as far as I could tell meant some of the seams had been ripped out or zippers had been put where God did not intend zippers to go) because gallery directors had to look like gallery directors, and having lunches at very expensive restaurants with curators and corporate art consultants or, occasionally, an actual artist. My mother had had a fairly successful career editing art books until she married her second husband, and apparently once you stop working legitimately it is impossible to start again. "Oh, I could never go back to that work, it's so dreary and the last thing the world needs is another coffee table book," I had heard her say more than once. When I asked her if she thought the world needed an aluminum garbage can decoupaged with pages torn from the King James Bible she said, No, the world didn't need that, which was exactly what made it art. And then I said, Well, if the world doesn't need coffee table books then they must be art, too—what was the difference? My mother said the difference was the world *thought* it needed coffee table books, the world *valued* coffee table books, but the world didn't think it needed decoupaged garbage cans.

And so Gillian and I were sitting in the kitchen, she intent on the crossword and I enjoying my fried egg sandwich, when we heard the front door unlocking—or actually locking, for we had carelessly left it unlocked, so it was first locked and then unlocked—which took a moment during which my sister and I just looked at each other and said nothing, for we instinctually knew who was opening the door. My father has keys to our apartment, and it would have made sense—well, more sense—that it was he arriving, seeing as how my mother was supposed to be honeymooning in Las Vegas, but for some reason both Gillian and I knew immediately it was our mother. We heard her drag her rolling suitcase over the threshold (my mother does not travel lightly, especially on honeymoons) and then we heard it topple over, and then we heard her chucking the books and magazines and other debris that had accumulated on the couch in her absence to the floor, and then we heard her collapse on the couch, and say, rather quietly and poignantly, "Shit."

We sat there for a moment in stunned silence. It was almost as if we thought if we remained silent and undetected, she might reverse herself—get off the couch, replace the debris, right her suitcase, toddle it out the door, fly back to Las Vegas, and resume her honeymoon.

But of course that did not happen. After a moment we heard her get up and walk toward the kitchen.

"Oh good Lord," my mother said, when she entered the kitchen and saw us, "what are you two doing here?"

"What are you doing here?" asked Gillian.

My mother went to the sink and scowled disapprovingly at

the dirty dishes and glasses. She opened the cupboard that housed glasses, but it was empty, for Gillian and I had been favoring the technique of rinsing and reusing glasses rather than washing, storing, and reusing. "My God," my mother said, "all I want is a drink of water. A simple drink of water! That is all I want. And that, like everything else I have ever wanted, appears to be denied me."

Gillian arose and found a fairly clean glass in the sink and rinsed it and then filled it with water from the tap. "Here," she said, and handed it to our mother.

"Bless you," my mother said. My mother is not a religious person and her use of this language disquieted me. Or further disquieted me, as her unexpected arrival had already achieved that effect.

"Whatever," Gillian said, and sat back down.

My mother stood at the sink, taking odd, birdlike sips from the glass of water. I thought about how I had once learned that birds cannot swallow and so must tip their heads back to ingest water, and how if in a rainstorm their beaks are left open and their heads tilted back they will drown, although why they would have their beaks open and heads thrown back during a rainstorm is a mystery to me. My mother finally finished drinking her water in this odd manner and then made what seemed to me to be a great show of rinsing out the glass and putting it in the dishwasher, which of course was not an easy thing to do as the dishwasher was already full of (dirty) dishes.

"What happened?" asked Gillian.

"What happened?"

"Yes," said Gillian. "Why are you home? Where is Mr. Rogers?" Both my sister and I enjoyed calling our mother's new husband by his surname, even though we had been urged repeatedly to call him Barry.

"I neither know nor care to know where that man is," my mother said. "I hope that I never see Barry again in my life."

"Well, best to discover that now," said Gillian. "Although I suppose it would have been best to discover that before you married him. Or before you agreed to marry him. Or before you met him."

"Gillian!" my mother said. "Please."

"It's Gillian," said Gillian.

"What?" my mother asked.

"My name is Gillian," said Gillian. "My name has been mispronounced long enough. I have decided that from now on I will only answer to Gillian. Rainer Maria says naming a child and then mispronouncing that name is a subtle and insidious form of child abuse."

"Well, that's not my style. If I were going to abuse you, there'd be nothing subtle or insidious about it." My mother looked at me. "And you," she said, "why aren't you at the gallery?"

"John didn't need me today," I said.

"That is not the point," said my mother. "John never needs you. You do not go there because you are needed. You go there because I pay you to go there so you will have a summer job and learn the value of a dollar and know what responsibility is all about."

"I'll go tomorrow," I said.

My mother sat at the table. She took the half-finished crossword puzzle away from Gillian. "Please remove that plate," she said to me. "There is nothing more disgusting than a plate on which a fried egg sandwich has been eaten." My mother is very particular about what people around her eat. She cannot stand to watch anyone eat a banana, unless they peel the whole thing and break it into attractive bite-sized pieces.

I got up and rinsed the plate and put it in the dishwasher. I filled the dishwasher with detergent and started the cycle. This act was too transparently ingratiating for anyone to acknowledge, yet it seemed to have a softening effect upon my mother: she sighed and rested her head on her arms, which were crossed before her on the table.

"What happened?" asked Gillian.

My mother did not answer. I realized she was crying. Gillian stood up and moved behind her, reached down and embraced her, and held her while she sobbed.

I went down the hall into the living room and called John in Amagansett. A woman answered the phone. "Hello?" she said.

"Hello. Is John Webster there?"

"Who's calling?" the woman asked, in a hostile, challenging fashion intended no doubt to discourage telemarketers.

"This is Bryce Canyon," I said. I always refuse to give my real name when someone demands to know "Who's calling?" They should say "May I ask who's calling?" or "May I tell him who's calling?"

"He's not available at the moment, Mr. Canyon. Can I give him a message?"

"Yes," I said. "You may. Please tell Mr. Webster that Marjorie Dunfour has returned unexpectedly from her honeymoon and if Mr. Webster values his livelihood he should return to the city posthaste."

"Post what?" the woman asked.

"Haste," I said. "Posthaste. Without delay. Immediately."

"Perhaps you'd better talk to him yourself."

"I thought he was unavailable."

"He was," said the woman, "but he has appeared."

After a moment John said, "Hello."

"John, it's me," I said.

"James," he said. "What's up?"

"My mother is here," I said. "She just arrived. I thought you might like to know."

"Oh shit," he said. "What happened?"

"I'm not sure," I said, "but Mr. Rogers seems to be history."

"Oh, the poor thing," said John. "So soon. Well, I suppose it's all for the best, to figure it out sooner than later."

"That is what we told her," I said.

"All right," he said. "I'll take the jitney back tonight. You don't think she'll call the gallery this afternoon, do you? Or, God forbid, go in?"

"I doubt it. She seems preoccupied with her misfortune."

"You're so heartless, James. It's unnatural. I worry for you."

"I think you should worry about yourself. If she finds out you closed the gallery she might get a little heartless herself."

"I'm on my way," said John. "I'm packing my bags as we speak."

✦ ✦ ✦

I thought that under the circumstances the best thing to do might be to get out of the house, so I took our dog, a black standard poodle named Miró, to the dog run in Washington Square. Miró, who seems to think he is human, doesn't really enjoy the dog run, but he will sit patiently on the bench beside me, observing the simple canine ways of the other dogs with amused condescension.

Right outside of our building is a tree well filled with impatiens and English ivy with two plaques attached to the little iron trellis around its base. One reads IN MEMORY OF HOWARD MORRIS SHULEVITZ, BLOCK PRESIDENT 1980–1993. HE LOVED THIS BLOCK. When I first saw this plaque, about six years ago when my parents divorced (my mother sold the apartment we lived in on West Seventy-ninth Street and we moved downtown; my father moved into an awful Trump building on the Upper East Side. He has one of those hideous apartments with huge curved windows you can't open and fake gold faucets and weird men in costumes in the elevator in case you don't know how to push a button), I misinterpreted it, thinking that the dates supplied were Howard Morris Shulevitz's dates of birth and death, and that he had been a little boy who had died some tragic early death and as a consequence had been given the posthumous honorific title of Block President. I had very tender feelings about the boy, who had died at approximately the age I was then, and felt in some way that I must be his successor, and so I vowed to love the block with Howard's ardency, and I even had fantasies about dying young myself—I thought about throwing myself

out our living room window so that I would land on the sidewalk in front of the tree well. I would get my own plaque then,
beside Howard's: JAMES DUNFOUR SVECK, SECOND BLOCK PRES-
IDENT, 1985–1997. HE LOVED THIS BLOCK TOO. I made the
mistake of mentioning this little fantasy to my mother, who
informed me that Howard Morris Shulevitz had probably been
an old man, a petty tyrant who had nothing better to do than an-
noy his neighbors with building code violations. The second
plaque on the trellis emphatically states CURB YOUR DOG. I don't
remember exactly when this one was appended to the railing, but
one can only imagine why it was necessary, and now seeing those
adjacent plaques never fails to depress me, for even if Howard
Morris Shulevitz was, as per my mother's imagining, an unpleasant person, did he really deserve to have his name, and memory,
evoked beside a CURB YOUR DOG sign? I find this whole phenom-
enon of naming things after the deceased disconcerting. I don't
like to sit on a bench that is a memorial to someone's life. It
seems disrespectful. I think if you want to memorialize someone you should either erect a proper memorial, like the Lincoln
Memorial, or leave well enough alone.

The dog run is this area of the park that is completely
fenced, and once you pass through the two gates, which upon
penalty of death must never be simultaneously opened, you can
let your dog off the leash and let it frolic with its own kind.
When I arrived at about four o'clock, it was fairly empty. The
people who didn't have real jobs who frequented the dog run
during the day had left, and the people who had real jobs hadn't
yet arrived. This left a few dog walkers with a motley assortment

of dogs, all of whom seemed not in the mood to frolic. Miró
trotted to our favorite bench, which was, thankfully, by this time
of the day in the shade, and jumped up onto it. I sat beside him,
but he turned away and ignored me. In the privacy of our home,
Miró is a very affectionate creature, but in public he behaves like
a teenager who has no interest in a parent's affection. I assume he
thinks that it interferes with his I-am-not-a-dog pose.

There is a sense of camaraderie in the dog run that I hate.
This sort of smug friendliness dog owners share that they feel
entitles them to interact. If I was sitting on a bench in the park
proper, no one would approach me, but in the dog run it's as if
you are on some distant weirdly friendly planet. "Oh, is that a
standard poodle?" people will ask, or "Is it a he or a she?" or some
other idiotic question. Fortunately the dog walkers, professionals
that they are, only talk to one another, in the same way I have
noticed that nannies and mothers never interact in the play-
ground: each, like the dog walkers and dog owners, sticks to its
kind. And so Miró and I were left alone. Miró watched the other
dogs for a moment and then sighed and slowly lowered himself
down upon the bench, pushing me a bit with his hind feet so
that he would have adequate space to recline. But I refused to
shift, so he was forced to hang his head over the end of the
bench. He did this in a way that implied it was very difficult being a dog.

I thought about my mother and her unexpected return. I
wasn't surprised that this marriage failed—there had been something weird about Mr. Rogers from the start, which was only
eight months ago—but I had thought it would last longer than a

few days. My mother was married to my father for fifteen years, and she was married to her second husband for three years, so I suppose this marriage was proportionate. I tried to figure out what percentage of fifteen years three years was so I could figure out what the corresponding percentage of three years would be—might it be four days? Unfortunately I have never been good in math. Numbers simply do not interest me or seem as real to me as words.

But whether it was proportionate or not, four days is still a disappointingly short time for a marriage to endure. And one could argue that the curve should be just the opposite—that people should get better with subsequent marriages, not worse. At this rate, my mother would be abandoned at the altar if she dared wed again.

My father has never remarried—the woman he left my mother for died, suddenly and tragically, of ovarian cancer before they could both divorce and remarry, cancer moving more expeditiously than the court system, and although he is not religious (my parents were married in the Rainbow Room by a judge) I think he felt in some way punished by this death, and since then he has been involved briefly with a long string of much younger women who all seem to have the same artificial-looking blond "highlights" in their perfectly nice brown hair. (I don't know if this is a generational thing or a fetish of my father's.)

That evening my mother went to consult with Hilda Temple, her life coach. My mother had been in conventional therapy for many years (in fact she had spent the last couple of years in analysis), but shortly before she met Mr. Rogers, she decided that conventional therapy wasn't "working for her" and had begun to see a life coach. What you did was tell your life coach what your goals were and your life coach would encourage/pester you until you achieved said goals or (more likely) moved on to a different form of therapy. Meeting Mr. Rogers had been one of my mother's goals—well, not meeting Mr. Rogers specifically, and in retrospect certainly not Mr. Rogers; the goal had been to find a partner—and with Hilda's help (or interference) this had been quickly achieved.

While my mother was out Gillian filled me in on what she had learned. Apparently Mr. Rogers had stolen my mother's ATM and credit cards, or at least "borrowed" them while she lay dozing in her nuptial bed, and somehow used them to get $3,000, all of which he successfully gambled away in the wee small hours of the morning. (Later, when she got her credit card bill, she learned that he had also bought several lap dances—discreetly billed as a "personal entertainment expense"—a $1,500 portable cigar humidor, $800 worth of cigars, and a dozen pairs of cashmere socks.)

I was in my bedroom when my mother returned from her summit meeting with Hilda Temple. Gillian had gone uptown to see Herr Schultz. For a while I could hear my mother in the living room talking to Miró. I've always been a bit jealous of how much my mother talks to the dog. In fact, I think we all talk to Miró more than we talk to one another. Then I heard her walking down the hall. I was sitting at my desk, looking up houses for sale in small midwestern towns on the Internet. It's amazing what $100,000 can get you in a state like Nebraska. I heard my mother stop in my doorway but I didn't look up.

"Oh, you're home," she said.

Since this was obvious I saw no point in either confirming or denying it.

"I thought you might be out," she said. "Shouldn't you be out?"

"Out where?"

"I don't know: out. At a party or something. Or a movie. You're eighteen and it's Friday night."

"Thursday night."

"Whatever," she said. "You should still be out. I worry about you. What are you doing?"

"Looking at houses."

"Houses? What houses?"

"Houses for sale."

"Isn't that an odd thing to be doing? I didn't know you were in the market for a house."

"I'm not," I said. "I'm just looking."

She stood there for a moment.

I turned around. "What are you doing?" I asked.

"Just looking at you," she said. "You'll be gone before I know it."

I'm supposed to be going to Brown University in Rhode Island this fall. Well, actually next month: there's some awful freshman-orientation thing at the end of August. I dread it.

My mother sat down on my bed.

"I'm sorry about Mr. Rogers," I said. "Gillian told me what happened."

My mother said nothing.

"What did Hilda have to say?" I asked.

She looked up at me, and rubbed her eyes. She looked tired and old, in a way I have never seen her look tired and old. "I'd rather not talk about Mr. Rogers," she said.

"Okay," I said. "Well, I'm sorry."

My mother reached out and gently wiped my cheek as if there was a smudge or something on it, but I knew it was only an excuse to touch me. "I'm so tired," she said. "I don't think I've been this tired in all my life."

"Then you should go to bed."

In lieu of an answer, my mother lay down on my bed. I turned back to my computer. I was looking at a house in Roseville, Kansas. It was beautiful. It was an old stone house with gables and a dumbwaiter and the original porcelain claw-foot tubs. It had a pantry and a screened sleeping porch. It had a stone basement that had been a stop on the Underground Railroad.

"Look at this," I said.

My mother sighed and sat up. "What?" she said.

"This," I said. "Come over here."

She got up and leaned over my shoulder. She smelled a little odd. I could smell Prélasser, her favorite perfume, but there was another odor just beneath it, an odd, harsh odor of exhaustion or panic or despair. "What?" my mother said again.

"Look at this house," I said. "Isn't it beautiful?"

"Where is it?" my mother asked.

"Kansas," I said. "Look at these pictures." I began to click through the photographs that were posted: the living room, the dining room, the kitchen, the central hallway and staircase, the bathroom, the bedrooms.

"Isn't it nice?" I asked.

"I don't like those old houses," my mother said.

"I do," I said. "It has a sleeping porch. And a dumbwaiter. And a Tiffany-glass window."

"Who'd want to sleep on a porch?" my mother asked.

"I would," I said.

"You'd get eaten alive by bugs. There are lots of awful bugs out there in the Midwest."

"It's screened in," I said.

"I'd feel like I was in a cage," said my mother. "And people could see in. Besides, what's wrong with air-conditioning?" She stood up and sighed and said, "Well. I suppose I'm going to bed." But she stood there, as if she wanted to be contradicted.

After a moment I said, "Why did you marry him?"

She didn't answer. She was looking out the window, or perhaps only looking at her reflection in the window—I couldn't tell. For a moment I thought perhaps I had not actually asked the question, only thought it. But then she shook her head lightly, as if to clear it. She was still facing the dark window. "Because I was lonely," she said.

I didn't know what to say. I said nothing.

"It gets lonely," she continued. She seemed to be in some kind of trance, speaking to her reflection in the window. "Even with you, and Gillian when she deigns to honor us with her presence, and Miró, and my friends, and the gallery, and lunches and dinners and brunches. He was lovely to sleep with, it was lovely to have someone hold me at night." She paused. "Oh," she said. "I shouldn't be telling you any of this."

"Why not?"

She turned away from the window. "I'll warp you. I'll pass all my bitterness and skepticism on to you, and you won't believe in love."

"I already don't believe in love."

"Of course you don't. How could you? You've never been in love. Or have you? Have I missed something?"

"No," I said.

"You will," she said.

"No I won't," I said.

She put her two hands on my shoulders and bent down and kissed my cheek. "You're too sweet not to fall in love. I know how sweet you are. Maybe better than anyone."

"I'm not sweet," I said.

"Hush," my mother said. "Don't contradict me. I'm exhausted. I'm going to bed. Just say good night."

She stood in the doorway. I turned around in my chair. "Good night," I said.

She walked down the hall, and then turned the hall light off. I heard her bedroom door open and then close. I heard a noise behind me, a little ping from the computer. I turned around: because I hadn't touched a key in five minutes, the monitor had shut itself off. The house in Roseville, Kansas, had disappeared, replaced by the dark reflection of my face.

2

Friday, July 25, 2003

ABOUT ONE THING, AT LEAST, MY MOTHER WAS RIGHT: JOHN did not need me at the gallery. In fact he probably could have got more work done without me there, because we liked each other and spent a lot of time talking. I did have a few duties: I was responsible for removing the detritus that collected in the garbage cans at the end of each day. People delighted in treating these $16,000 works of art as ordinary waste receptacles, which is exactly how the artist desired the viewer to "interface" with them. Mostly I would find coins (people have this urge to literally throw their money away; I don't get it), used Kleenex, candy wrappers, but occasionally people were more creative: I also found a used condom and a soiled diaper. Since I assumed the sexual or excretory acts that produced these items did not occur in the gallery, it meant that people had brought these contributions with them, and I found such attempts at creativity a little disturbing.

The artist who created the garbage cans had no name. He was Japanese, and had interesting theories about identity—for a while, earlier in his career, he had changed his name every month, for he felt identity was fluid and should not be constrained by something as fixed as a name. But apparently after a while of changing his name every month people lost track, and then lost interest in learning, or remembering, his name. So he divested himself of names completely. I think part of my mother's irritation with Gillian's reconsideration of her name had to do with her experience with this artist. Originally she had thought that an artist without a name who worked with garbage cans and sacred texts would attract a lot of publicity, but his not having a name made him somewhat difficult to promote, and her excitement had turned to frustration. None of the garbage cans had sold, and my mother attributed this to the lack of media exposure, or "buzz," as she liked to call it. She pleaded with the artist without a name to be referred to as "The Artist Without a Name," or "No-Name," or something buzzy like that, but he refused, reasoning that those were, in and of themselves, names.

I was supposed to keep all the things I collected in a separate garbage can in the storeroom, because he claimed his next project would be to make art of this refuse. (My mother made me throw the used condom and diaper out, for obvious reasons.) My other tasks in the gallery were to keep the mailing list updated, which meant entering the names and addresses people wrote in the guest book on the counter. As few people visited the gallery on those baked summer days, and many who did visit did not sign the book, updating the mailing list was not an onerous task. Every morning I brought John a cappuccino, a double-berry yogurt muffin, two 36-ounce bottles of Evian water, *The New York Times*, the *Post*, and, depending on which day it was, either *The New Yorker*, *New York*, *Time Out*, or *The New York Observer*. (John refused to subscribe to newspapers and magazines because he thought the address labels affixed to them were aesthetically compromising.)

If John wasn't having lunch with someone, which he tried very hard to do every day, I was sent out to fetch him the salad platter from Fabu, the chic food boutique around the corner on Tenth Avenue. Every day they offered a variety of about a dozen salads, from which you could pick a selection of three for $11.95, which included iced tea or iced coffee and a hunk of artisanal bread. (This bread was not sliced but "hand-torn"; apparently slicing adversely affected its taste and texture.) Fabu released its menu to the world via fax at 11:00 a.m. every day, and deciding which three out of the twelve salads to select occupied the better part of John's morning. And finally, about four o'clock in the afternoon, I would be sent out to fetch him an iced cappuccino and a dark chocolate Milky Way bar.

If I wasn't maintaining John's sugar and caffeine levels, and there was someone in the gallery (which was seldom), I would sit behind the counter and type quickly and efficiently on the computer, thus giving the appearance that business was thriving, or if not thriving, at least occurring. And answer people's questions or provide information about the art, or the artist, but when people asked questions they usually wanted to know the address of another gallery or if they could use the bathroom.

The rest of the time I sat around and talked with John, who never seemed to do much of anything. I liked John very much. In fact, except for my grandmother, he was really the only person I liked. John had grown up in Georgia and graduated from high school when he was sixteen with perfect SAT scores. He went to Harvard on a full scholarship, which required him to work for the university. His junior year he was given a job as a security guard in the Fogg Museum and was quickly promoted to tour guide when it became evident that he could answer many of the questions that stumped the other guides. John loved art, mostly painting. He said he never saw a real painting, a good painting, until he went to Harvard, but all through his childhood he would look at art book after art book, and he basically taught himself the entire history of art. After Harvard he got a master's degree from the Courtauld Institute in London. He managed the art collection of my father's law firm before my mother lured him away. (Why law firms have multimillion-dollar art collections is a mystery to me.)

When I arrived the Friday morning after my mother's unexpected return, John was already at the gallery, which was unusual. He sat at his desk in his private office, and he appeared to be actually working, although what he could be doing, I had no idea. I gave him his cappuccino, his muffin, and one bottle of Evian water (the other went into the refrigerator).

"You're here early," I said.

"Yes," he said. "I wanted to make sure I was here in case your mother appeared. And being away for a few days creates work. Lots of faxes and e-mails to answer." He pointed to the mess on his desk.

"Anything I can do?" I asked.

"Is the mailing list up-to-date?"

"Yes," I said. "Unless people broke in while we were gone and left their names and addresses."

"We'll have no snarkiness today, thank you very much," said John. "So tell me, what happened?"

I sat down on one of the two Le Corbusier chairs that faced his desk. "Apparently Mr. Rogers is a compulsive gambler. He stole my mother's credit cards and lost about three thousand dollars."

"Three thousand dollars? That's all? Some of my dates cost me nearly that much. I don't think it's anything to end a marriage over."

"It's not really the amount. I think it's more the issue of trust. He waited till she was sleeping and took her cards and left. On the third night of their honeymoon."

"Well, I admit it's bad behavior. And what a shame. Now she'll want to throw herself back into the gallery. Women who are spurned always turn their attention to work. I was looking forward to a nice long quiet summer. Is she coming in today?"

"I don't know. She was still in bed when I left."

"Well, we will just have to wait and see. There is a lot of mail. I left it on the counter. Why don't you open it and sort it?"

"Okay," I said.

John pried the sippy lid off his cappuccino. "What's wrong with this?" he asked.

"What? Nothing's wrong with it."

"Are you sure you asked for 2 percent?"

"Yes," I said.

He sniffed it. "It doesn't look right. It has that nasty skim look."

"It's 2 percent," I said. "I'm sure."

"All right," he said. "Now go do some work. We must look very busy at all times today."

I left his office and sat behind the front counter. There was a big stack of mail piled there, and I began to sort through it. About eleven o'clock, just as the Fabu menu was being spit out of the fax machine, John emerged from his office. He had an uncanny ability to sense exactly when the Fabu fax would arrive, and was usually standing above the machine as it emerged.

"Damn," he said. "I was really in the mood for the Thai peanut and mango salad. It's not here. Don't they usually have it on Fridays?"

"I don't know," I said.

"I really want it," said John. "I've been craving it all morning. Maybe they just forgot to list it. Why don't you call and ask if they have it."

"I'm sure if they had it, it would be on the menu," I said.

"Well, just call and make sure." He walked back into his office, still studying the menu.

Since I knew that if Fabu were offering the Thai peanut and mango salad they would list it on their menu, I did not call to confirm the obvious. I waited a moment and went into John's office and gave him the bad news. "Fuck," he said. "Why do they put me through this? Why can't they just serve the same goddamned salads every day? This is insane. What are you getting for lunch?"

"It's Friday," I said. "I'm having lunch with my father." Every Friday I had a standing appointment to have lunch with my father downtown.

"Oh, that's right," said John. "So I'm stuck here. Well, I'll have the baby spinach and pear, the orzo with olives and sun-dried tomatoes, and I guess the tomato, basil, and mozzarella."

"And what do you want to drink?" I asked.

"Oh," said John. He sighed, as if I was making things very difficult for him. "Get me the ginger lemonade if they have it. If not, the mint iced tea. And will you go pick it up? When they deliver it takes forever and all the salads get mushed together. I hate it when they get mushed together."

"I'm going downtown," I said.

"I know," he said. "It will only take a minute. Please. And carry it carefully so it doesn't get mushed."

"All right," I said. "But I'll have to leave early."

"Go whenever you want," said John.

It used to be very easy to visit my father at his office: you just walked through the lobby, got on the elevator, and took it up to the forty-ninth floor. But since 9/11 you have to stand on a line in the lobby and then show a guard a picture I.D. If your name is on the list of expected guests, you can then proceed to the elevators. If it isn't, you have to go to another line and tell that guard who you are visiting and wait while he calls that person and gets permission for you to enter. My father invariably forgets to put me on the list of expected guests ("I'm too busy to remember things like that," he told me; I asked him if he could instruct his assistant to put me on the list, but his assistant has worked for him so long—about twenty years, I think—that he no longer thinks of himself as an assistant and refuses to do any petty clerical tasks, and since basically his job is composed of only petty clerical tasks, he does very little), so it always takes me about fifteen or twenty minutes to get from the lobby up to his office, and then I have to announce myself to the receptionist and wait until my father appears to collect me, for I am not trusted to walk unescorted down the hallway to his office.

I sat in the reception area, and while I waited for my father a woman appeared from the interior and signed herself out at the reception desk. She looked at me and smiled.

"Are you Jim Bigley's son?" she asked.

"No," I said. "I'm Paul Sveck's son."

She immediately stopped smiling as if I had said I was the son of Adolf Hitler. I wondered what my father had done to alienate her. While I was pondering this, Myron Axel, my father's so-called assistant, appeared and beckoned for me to follow him. Myron Axel is a strange man. In the many years he has worked for my father he has never revealed any aspect of his personal life. One might assume this is because he is a private person, but it seems much more likely, upon meeting him, that he has no private life to reveal. Myron Axel walks very strangely, sort of keeping his body stiff and only moving his feet, as if any more movement might have been unseemly. I followed him down the long hallway, past big windowed offices on one side and small windowless offices on the other. I don't think I could ever work in such a blatantly hierarchical corporate setting. I know that everyone in this world is not equal, but I can't bear environments that make this truth so obvious. My father's sun-filled corner office has an amazing view, a Diebenkorn (thanks to John Webster), a vintage Florence Knoll desk, a leather sofa (Le Corbusier, of course), and a saltwater aquarium, while Myron Axel works in a fluorescently lit closet across the hall.

My father was on the telephone but motioned for me to enter. "Thank you," I said to Myron, who did not acknowledge this remark. I went into my father's office and looked out the window at the view, which is always changing with the season, with the light, with the time of day. It is the only time I'm aware of living in a big city, when I visit my father's office—the rest of the time, being down in it, at ground level, the notion of it somehow disappears.

"I know you're lying and these are stupid, time-wasting lies," my father said. "They're not even interesting. When you're ready to talk sensibly, call me back." He hung up the phone.

"Hello, James," he said. "I'm glad you're wearing a jacket and tie. Even though it looks as if you slept in them. I thought we might pop up to the partners' dining room." My father much prefers to eat in the partners' dining room because it's quicker and cheaper than any of the restaurants downtown, but he always pretends he is doing it to please me: as if eating in a room full of suits is a big thrill.

But I like my father, even though he is annoying and silly. It is hard not to like him: he is so handsome and charming. He grew up in a working-class family in New Bedford, Massachusetts, and he has never grown inured to his success. He goes to London once a year to buy his suits, his shoes are made in Italy from a plaster cast of his foot, his underwear comes from Switzerland, and his shirts are custom-made by a tailor in Chinatown. He takes great delight in all these extravagances. He is happy and generous.

He drummed on his desk and stood up. "Shall we go? I have to be back here for a conference call at two."

I followed him out of the office. He stopped outside the door to Myron's closet and said, "If Dewberry calls get an address we can FedEx the papers to." He didn't wait for Myron to reply, but I suppose that is because Myron rarely does. He walked briskly down the long hallway, and I followed behind him.

We were given a table along the windows, looking out at New York Harbor, the Statue of Liberty, and Governors Island. There was a big empty place in the sky to the right of us, and we could see parts of New Jersey and the Hudson River that had previously been obscured. I tried not to look out that way.

"Have you heard from Mom?" I asked.

"No," he said. "Why would I hear from your mother? Isn't she on one of her honeymoons?" My father always likes to imply that my mother marries frequently and indiscriminately, although she has only married thrice.

"No," I said. "She came home yesterday."

"I thought she was away until the twenty-ninth."

"Supposedly. But her plans changed."

"Why? What happened?"

"Mr. Rogers stole her credit cards and gambled away about three thousand dollars."

My father guffawed, tried to turn it into a cough, and drank from his water glass.

"It isn't funny," I said.

"I know," he said. "Of course it isn't funny. It's just that—well, this is why you should never get married, James. There's no reason for a man to get married anymore. Women will make you think so, but believe me, there's not. No goddamn reason whatsoever."

"Well, I don't plan to get married," I said.

"Good," said my father. "Glad to hear it."

The waiter came over for our order. My father ordered steak and I ordered penne with basil and heirloom tomatoes.

"You should have ordered a steak or something," my father said. "You should never order pasta as a main course. It isn't manly."

"I'll keep that in mind," I said.

"No, you won't," said my father. "And listen, while we're talking about this, let me ask you something."

"What?"

"Are you gay?"

"What?" I asked. "Why would you ask me that?"

"Why? Why not? I just want to know."

"Why? Do you get to take an extra deduction on your taxes or something?"

"Very funny, James. No. It's just that we've never talked about your sexuality, and if you are gay I want to be properly supportive. It's fine with me if you're gay, I just want to know."

"You wouldn't be supportive if I were straight?"

"Of course I would. But not—well, the world supports heterosexuals. It's the norm. Heterosexuals don't really need support. But gays do. So I'd have to make a special effort. That's all I want to know. Should I be making a special effort? Should I not say things about pasta being faggy?"

"I don't really care what you say," I said.

"Be that as it may, I would still like to know what is right and wrong for me to say."

"Dad, if you're homophobic I don't want you to change for my sake."

"I'm not homophobic! James! I just said I wouldn't care if you were gay. It wouldn't bother me a bit."

"Well then, why can't I eat pasta as a main course?"

"Because that's not gay—I never said it was gay. I said it was not manly."

This inane conversation was interrupted by one of my father's colleagues, Mr. Dupont, who stopped by our table on his way out of the dining room. I had met Mr. Dupont a few times over the years.

"Hello, Paul," he said to my father. "Hello, James."

"Hi, Mr. Dupont."

"So your dad tells me you're headed off to Yale."

"Brown," I said. "I think."

"Oh yes—Brown. Fine school, Brown. Huck's off to Dartmouth. Turned down a full hockey scholarship at University of Minnesota. Imagine what that would have saved me."

"A bundle," said my father.

"A bundle and a half," said Mr. Dupont. "Well, gentlemen, enjoy your lunch. I hope you're getting the steak. It's excellent today."

We sat for a moment in silence, and then the waiter delivered our meals. My father glanced at my plate of pasta, but said nothing. He cut into his nearly raw beef and smiled at the blood it drooled. "So," he said, after he had taken a bite, "you're not going to tell me?"

"Not going to tell you what?"

"Whether or not you're gay."

"No," I said. "Why should I? Did you tell your parents?"

"I wasn't gay," said my father. "I was straight."

"So, what, if you're gay you have a moral obligation to inform your parents and if you're straight you don't?"

"James, I'm just trying to be helpful. I'm just trying to be a good father. You don't have to get hostile. I just thought you might be gay, and if you were, I wanted to let you know that's fine, and help you in whatever way I could."

"Why might you think I was gay?"

"I don't know. You just seem—well, let's put it this way: you don't seem interested in girls. You're eighteen, and as far as I know you've never been on a date."

I said nothing.

"Am I wrong? Or is that true?"

"Just because I've never been on a date doesn't mean I'm gay. And besides, no one goes on dates anymore."

"Well, whatever—normal kids hang out. They go out. Maybe *date* isn't the right word, but you know what I mean."

"You don't think I'm normal?"

"James, both of us know you have never been normal. We don't need to argue about that. Now let's drop the subject. I've obviously struck a nerve. I'm sorry. I was only trying to help you."

I didn't say anything.

My father attacked his steak with virility. I daintily ate my pasta. After a moment he said, "What do you mean, 'I think'?"

"What?"

"You told Mr. Dupont that you're going to Brown, 'I think.'"

"Oh, well, I'm not sure."

"What do you mean you're not sure? Of course you're going to Brown. We've already sent them money. You can't switch schools now."

"I wasn't thinking of switching schools," I said.

"Good," said my father.

"I'm thinking of not going to college at all."

My father put down his knife and fork. "What?" he said.

"I'm not sure I want to go to college. In fact, I'm pretty sure I don't."

"What do you mean, you don't want to go to college? Of course you want to go to college. What do you want to do, run away and join the circus?"

"I don't know. Maybe. I just don't want to go to college."

"Why? Why not?"

"I think it would be a waste of time."

"A waste of time! College?"

"Yes," I said. "For me. I'm confident I can teach myself everything I want to know by reading books and seeking out the knowledge that interests me. I don't see the point of spending four years—four very expensive years—learning a lot of stuff I'm not particularly interested in and am bound to forget, just because it's the social norm. And besides, I can't bear the idea of spending four years in close proximity with college students. I dread it."

"What's so bad about college students?"

"They'll all be like Huck Dupont."

"You've never met Huck Dupont."

"I don't need to meet him. The fact that his name is Huck and he got a full hockey scholarship to the University of Minnesota is enough for me."

"What's wrong with hockey?"

"Nothing," I said, "if you like blood sport. But I don't think people should get full scholarships to state universities because they're psychopaths."

"Well, forget Huck Dupont. He's going to Dartmouth. You're going to Brown. I doubt they even have a hockey team."

"Whether Brown has a hockey team or not is not the point.

The point is I don't want to spend a huge amount of your money doing something that has no value or meaning to me. In fact, I think it's obscene to pay thousands of dollars for me to go to college when there are so many people living in poverty in the world."

"James, the fact that poverty exists is not a good reason for you not to go to college. And the existence of poverty does not prevent you from doing other foolish and extravagant things, like eating an eighteen-dollar bowl of pasta."

"This didn't cost eighteen dollars," I said.

"It would if we were paying market rate."

"Well, if that's foolish and extravagant, why isn't going to college foolish and extravagant?"

"Because college is an investment in your future. It doesn't pass through your digestive system in twenty-four hours. But, James, you're just being silly. You're going to college. You'll love college. You're a very intelligent young man. I know high school has been a bit difficult and boring for you, but college is different. You'll be challenged and stimulated, believe me."

"Why must everyone go to college?"

"Not everyone goes to college," my father said. "In fact, very few people go to college. It's a privilege to spend four years in the pursuit of knowledge. I would think it would be just the thing for someone like you."

"I don't see it that way. I think I can learn all I need and want to know by reading Shakespeare and Trollope."

"So what do you propose to do? Sit at home and read Trollope for four years?"

"No," I said. "I want to buy a house."

"A house? Are you crazy? Do you have any idea what houses cost?"

"I don't mean in New York City. I mean in Indiana. Or Kansas. Or South Dakota. Someplace like that."

"And where will you get this money to buy a house?"

"If you gave me a third of the money you're going to spend sending me to Brown I could easily make a substantial down payment on a very nice home."

"And what would you do in this very nice home in Kansas? Read Trollope?"

"Yes," I said, "among other things. I'd also want to work."

"At the local McDonald's, I presume?"

"Maybe. Why not?"

"James, your mother and I did not raise you to work at Mc-Donald's in Kansas. We raised you to be an educated and accomplished person. If after four years in college you feel you would like to move to Kansas and work in a McDonald's, that is your decision to make. This is one thing about which both your mother and I agree. So we will stop talking about this now, because you're going to college, where you will flourish and be happy *and* read Shakespeare and Trollope."

I said nothing. We ate for a few moments in silence and then my father said, "So how is your mother? Is she okay?"

"I think so," I said. "She's just upset. And sad."

"Well, the good thing about your mother is she won't be sad for long."

I hate when my father makes remarks like this about my

mother or when my mother makes them about my father. I think that when you divorce someone you forfeit your right to comment on her actions or character. "What are you doing this weekend?" I asked my father. "Are you going to be at the beach?"

My parents had owned a house in East Hampton when they split up; my mother got the apartment in Manhattan and my father got the house at the beach. For the first few years Gillian and I had spent both July and August out there with him, but the last couple of years the arrangement was more informal, and we came and went as we—and my father—pleased.

"No," he said. "I'm staying in town this weekend."

"Why?" I asked.

"Nothing, really. I'm having a bit of minor surgery."

"Surgery? What's wrong?"

"Nothing's wrong."

"Then why are you having surgery?"

"It isn't really surgery. It's outpatient surgery. A very simple procedure. Nothing to worry about."

"Well, what is it? What are you doing?"

My father said nothing.

"Dad, what are you doing?"

"I'm having eye surgery," he said.

"Oh," I said. "Laser surgery?"

"Not exactly," he said.

"Then what are you having?"

"I'd rather not say, James. Suffice it to say I will not be at the house this weekend. You and Gillian are free to use it if you wish."

"Are you having plastic surgery?"

"No," said my father.

"Good," I said.

"Why good?"

"I don't know. I'd just feel very weird if you altered your appearance for reasons of vanity. I think you look fine, Dad, and you don't need any surgery."

"What about these bags under my eyes?" he asked.

"What bags?"

"These," he said, indicating the dark slightly protuberant bag beneath each of his eyes.

"Those aren't bags, Dad. Just get a good night's sleep. And stop eating meat. That's all you need to do."

"Well, they are bags and I'm having them fixed on Saturday. And it's none of your business."

"Wow, Dad," I said. "Plastic surgery."

"It's not called plastic surgery anymore. It's elective cosmetic surgery."

"Wow, Dad. Elective cosmetic surgery."

"It's not a big deal. Please don't tell Gillian or your mother. Listen, I should head back downstairs. I don't want to miss that conference call. Do you want dessert? You're welcome to stay and order some if you'd like."

"No thanks. I'm fine."

"All right, then," said my father. "Let's blow this pop stand."

In the subway uptown, on my way back to the gallery, I thought about what I had said to my father. I had no desire to go to college, and practically from the moment I was accepted at Brown, I had been trying to devise a feasible alternative plan, but it had seemed inevitable—not going to college was simply not an option I thought I had. After lunch with my father, I realized it was. It wouldn't be easy and it would piss my parents off, but I was eighteen, an adult, and they couldn't force me to go to college against my will.

The main problem was I don't like people in general and people my age in particular, and people my age are the ones who go to college. I would consider going to college if it were a college of older people. I'm not a sociopath or a freak (although I don't suppose people who are sociopaths or freaks self-identify as such); I just don't enjoy being with people. People, at least in my experience, rarely say anything interesting to each other. They always talk about their lives and they don't have very interesting lives. So I get impatient. For some reason I think you should only say something if it's interesting or absolutely has to be said. I had never really been aware of how difficult these feelings made things for me until an experience I had this spring.

A horrible experience.

3

April 2003

I WENT TO THIS SEMINAR THING IN WASHINGTON, D.C., called The American Classroom. Two students from every state were selected to participate and were carted off to Washington for a week. Every senior in my high school had to write an essay about some aspect of government or politics, and in an effort to ensure that I wouldn't be picked, I wrote what I thought was this very lame and silly essay about how I believed women make better government leaders than men, because women seem better able to think about others, and men—or at least men who seek power—seem able to think only about themselves: their wealth, their power, the size of their cock. Anyway, even though I do believe that, it was a stupid essay, but somehow I was selected. I didn't want to go—the program was allegedly bipartisan but the NRA or the DAR or some organization like that ran it, and I knew it would be awful. I'm an anarchist. I hate politics. I hate politics and I hate religion: I'm an atheist, too. If it weren't so tragic, I think it would almost be funny that religion is supposed to be this good force in the world, making people moral, and charitable, and kind. The majority of the world's conflicts, past and present, are all caused by religious intolerance. I could go on and on about this because I find it very upsetting, especially with things like 9/11, but I won't. The point is I didn't want to go to The American Classroom, I knew it would be a nightmare, but I was told I had to go. This was right about the time last fall that I was applying to colleges, and being selected for The American Classroom was supposedly a very big deal that would get me into Harvard and Yale. (It didn't.)

Of course I went with a bad attitude but it was genuinely awful right from the beginning. Actually the beginning was okay, before I got to D.C., that is. I took a train from Penn Station to Washington, and I love traveling on trains, even pathetic Amtrak. The *very* beginning was bad—I had to deal with going through the nightmare that is called Penn Station. The idea that there was once a beautiful and majestic building in New York City that I cannot experience because some men in the 1960s decided to tear it down (this is a good example of why women should be in positions of power—I seriously doubt women would have torn down the old Penn Station) infuriates me. At the new, improved Penn Station they don't announce the platform until about thirty seconds before the train departs, which means you have to stand around staring up at the (really ugly) signboard and then make this mad dash along with thousands of other people to the announced platform if you want to get a seat.

So the very beginning of my trip was unpleasant, but once I got on the train, and found a good seat in the quiet car where people were forbidden to listen to music and/or talk on cell phones, things were okay.

One of the most foreboding things about The American Classroom was the dress code. "Men" had to wear jackets, ties, non-denim pants, and leather shoes. "Ladies" had to wear dresses or dress slacks and "appropriate" blouses and leather shoes. I found it a little distressing that a program supposedly celebrating the wonder of democracy had this totalitarian approach to dressing.

So I was wearing my jacket and tie and leather shoes and appropriate pants and enjoying my last minutes of freedom on the train ride down there. In addition to the aforementioned costume, we were also required to wear name tags the entire time we were in Washington. We had been sent our tags so we could be wearing them when we arrived at whatever airport or bus or train station we arrived at. These name tags said THE AMERICAN CLASSROOM in red-white-and-blue-striped letters and beneath that, in black letters, our name and the state we represented. Mine was in my pocket, because I refused to put it on until the last possible moment.

When I got off the train at Union Station it suddenly occurred to me that I could just pass the group by unidentified and wander out by myself and have a lovely solitary week in Washington. My mother had given me her credit card "just in case" I needed it, so I would have no problem checking into a hotel. I could spend a lot of time at the National Gallery or just stay in my hotel room reading *Can You Forgive Her?*, which I had brought with me on the off chance that I might have some time in between the indoctrination sessions. I was thinking about this when I saw a large group of oddly attired young adults not far ahead. A woman dressed like a flight attendant stood in their midst, apparently checking names off a list on her clipboard. The students had their name tags on and stood around like cattle waiting to be slaughtered. I walked past them and out the front door and stood on the sidewalk. A cabby asked me if I needed a cab and I said no. I knew I had to put on my name tag and turn around, go back inside, and join that miserable group. I said to myself, There are things in your life that you don't want to do that you will have to do. You cannot always do and go what and where you please. That is not how life works. This is one of those times when you must do and go what and where you do not want to do or go. I was nervously fingering my name tag inside my jacket pocket, flipping the needlelike prong in and out of its catch. And then I stuck my finger hard against it, hard enough so that I knew it would draw blood, because I wanted to bleed. If I had to do this, I wanted to bleed doing this.

When the perky lady had ticked off all the names on her list, we were ushered out of Union Station and into a waiting van. The lady turned out to be a (Republican) congressman's wife named Susan Porter Wright; she was a volunteer for The American Classroom. She told us how much she looked forward to it every year, how wonderful it was to meet the brightest and most civic-minded students from across the nation. Despite the fact we were all wearing name tags, she had us go around and introduce ourselves. After that she ignored us, talking on her cell phone to a caterer about a luau-inspired birthday party for her husband at which she wanted to roast a pig in her backyard.

I knew we were all staying in a hotel, and I had pictured one of the nice hotels near the Mall, so I was a bit panicked when we drove quickly through Washington and got on the highway in the direction of Arlington, Virginia. None of the other students seemed to notice that we were about to be transported across state lines, which I believe is a federal offense. They all seemed very well adjusted and friendly, chattering about where they came from and where they were going to college and how excited they were to be in Washington, D.C. (briefly, for we had already left it behind), for The American Classroom. One girl actually said, "This is the most exciting thing I've ever done in my life," but she was from North Dakota, so it made some sense. One girl asked me where I was from and I said New York, which I had already said during the very recent introductions, and the girl said Oh, where in New York, and I said New York City, and she said her mother was born on Staten Island, and I said cool. I couldn't think of anything else to say.

We drove farther and farther away from Washington, D.C., and I was about to ask Mrs. Wright where we were going when we got off the highway and pulled into the parking lot of a TraveLodge. It was one of those hotels in the middle of nowhere, surrounded by about six different highways, that you pass by and wonder who would ever stay there and why. Places like that, which seem unconnected to life as we live it, really unnerve me. It reminded me of an unfortunate incident about a year ago (that actually, now that I come to think of it, prefigures the unfortunate incident I'm about to relate). I met my father in Los Angeles for a few days; he was there for business, and we stayed in a hotel from which you could see the Getty Museum, all white and pretty and reflecting sunshine on the top of a hill, and so the first afternoon while he took the rental car to a meeting downtown, I set out to walk to the Getty Museum. I thought this would be fairly easy since I could see it; it seemed merely a matter of going around the corner and up the hill. But it turns out you can't walk to the Getty. At one point the sidewalk just ended for no apparent reason and I was forced to walk on the shoulder of the road, where obviously I was not supposed to be walking because I almost got run over. Drivers in L.A. are not pedestrian-friendly; it's like they've never seen pedestrians before and they don't believe they're real, so they can drive past them at eighty miles an hour. The road I thought would take me to the Getty Museum only took me to an eight-lane freeway, which I knew I could not cross, even though I could see the Getty Museum right in front of me. Risking death, I retraced my steps and found the service entrance to the Getty, a road that went up the back side of the hill the museum was so coyly perched upon, but the guards in a booth at the entrance to the road said only vehicles were allowed on the service road: apparently human feet must never touch it. This seemed so absurd to me, and I was so hot and pissed off, that I got belligerent and started to walk up the road, and the guards came charging out of the booth with their assault rifles drawn and practically tackled me. They threatened to call the police, but I pleaded with them and they ended up taking my picture and made me sign a form that said I would never visit the Getty Museum under any circumstances ever again. (I've since had this fantasy that at some point in my life I'll be given some major award and the award ceremony will be at the Getty Museum and I'll have to decline the award and they will ask me why and I'll tell them it's because of their unenlightened policy concerning pedestrian access to the museum and they'll realize how stupid it is and build a walkway up to the museum and name it after me.)

The location of the TraveLodge was not its only drawback. In order to conserve money and foster camaraderie amongst participants, we were housed three to a room, and this meant that a cot was stuck in every room, and of course the democratic principle of first come, first served was in effect, and since I was the last guy to arrive it meant I got the cot.

The experience of living with two other guys in a hotel room was so traumatic I don't remember much about it. I know this is all very abnormal and neurotic of me and I should probably shut up and join the army, sleep in a room with dozens of men, be forced to shit in a doorless stall, and just get over myself, but I hadn't joined the army and all I wanted was a place to be alone. Being alone is a basic need of mine like food and water, but I realize it is not so for others. My roommates seemed to enjoy living in the same room in a farting, let's-smoke-dope kind of way and didn't seem to mind the fact that they were never alone. I only feel like myself when I am alone. Interacting with other people does not come naturally to me; it is a strain and requires effort, and since it does not come naturally I feel like I am not really myself when I make that effort. I feel fairly comfortable with my family, but even with them I sometimes feel this strain of not being alone.

The last time I had been faced with a communal living situation like this was the summer I was twelve and was sent to sailing camp. It was the summer my parents got divorced and they sent both Gillian and me away. Gillian was fifteen and got to go on a grand European tour with her friend Hilary Candlewood's family, but I was banished to sailing camp on Cape Cod. I think my parents had waited too long to set something up for me, so all the normal camps were full (not that they would have been much better). I found out later that Camp Zephyr wasn't even a normal sailing camp, but one of those camps advertised in the back of *The New York Times Magazine* (along with the military prep schools) that supposedly reform seriously troubled adolescents through the wonders of hard physical labor and the glories of nature. Even the motto of Camp Zephyr was sinister: "Be Patient and Tough; Someday This Pain Will Be Useful to You."

4

Friday, July 25, 2003

WHEN I ARRIVED BACK AT THE GALLERY JOHN WAS SITTING behind the front desk, but when he saw me he got up and went into his office, closing his door. I knew my mother had arrived because the temperature had dropped about twenty degrees. Among my mother's many interesting but misguided notions was the idea that keeping the gallery chilled like a meat locker would be good for business. This idea was the result of taking seriously an article she had read in the Style section of the *Times*, which maintained that, based upon a recent survey of the temperature of various emporia in New York City, a venue's exclusivity was in direct inverse proportion to its temperature: Bergdorf Goodman's 63°; Kmart 75°.

And so I put on the sweater I kept handy for such chilly times as these. I assumed my position behind the counter and looked at the computer monitor, which displayed the gallery's home page. John always returns to this page after he's been surf-ing, and I don't think he realizes that just by pressing the BACK key I can see what sites he's been visiting. They are usually a very interesting mix of the esoteric and the pornographic. After a few clicks I found myself at Gent4Gent.com, "where quality men find other quality men." I clicked back one more window and found what I assumed was John's profile, as there was a photo-graph of him standing on the deck of a beach house in an ob-scenely (yet flatteringly) tight-fitting bathing suit. His profile was titled "Black Narcissus" and read as follows: *GBM, 33, 5'10", 175. Successful, educated, cultured. Handsome, fit, hot. Looking for smart and funny men interested in sex and semantics. Likes: Paul Smith, Paul Cézanne, Paul Bowles. Dislikes: Starbucks, Star Jones, Star Wars. Up for discourse, dates, debauchery.*

This relentlessly alliterative profile was followed by a long list of favorites: book, movie, leisure activity, country, etc., etc. At the bottom was a section where one described one's perfect part-ner. John's dream man was white, 26–35 years old, had a college degree or higher, made at least $50,000/year, was between 5'7" and 6'7" and between 140 and 240 pounds, smooth (but not shaved), "gym-fit," liked the arts, baseball, sex, tolerated cats, dogs, and birds, did not smoke but drank "socially," and used drugs "sparingly, if at all," practiced safe sex "always," lived in Manhattan, was spiritual but not religious, Democratic, vege-tarian, versatile, and uncut.

Because there was nothing else to do, and because it was free to join Gent4Gent (although you had to pay for "premium ser-vices"), I created and posted a profile for John's perfect partner.

I felt a little like the guy who created Frankenstein, for the creature I devised did seem potentially monstrous: a 30-year-old hunky blond (6', 190) who worked in the Contemporary Art Department of Sotheby's, was half-French and half-American (I had a feeling John was a Francophile), had graduated from Stanford and done postgraduate work at the Sorbonne, had two Maine coon cats ("Peretti" and "Bugatti"), loved the Yankees and New York City Ballet, lived in Chelsea, and had an 8" uncut cock.

About fifteen minutes later two people, a middle-aged man and woman, entered the gallery. They ignored me and walked around the garbage cans in that crablike shuffle that people use to maneuver around a gallery. They peered intently at every garbage can and spoke softly and incessantly in German. After they had examined them all, they approached the desk. They looked rich and glamorous in a Germans-visiting-galleries kind of way. The man was wearing a fawn-colored suede jacket over a brown Comme des Garcons T-shirt; the woman wore a Marimekko sundress (backward) and espadrilles. They both wore sunglasses.

"What is the name of this artist who made the garbage?" the woman asked. I couldn't tell if she was using the word *garbage* for identification purposes or judgmentally.

"He has no name," I said.

"He has no name?"

"Yes," I said. "He has no name."

"But he must have a name. What is he called?"

"You may refer to him however you like," I said. "He believes that having a name influences your perception of his work. He believes names are encumbrances."

"Ah yes, I see," she said. She said something in German to the man, who nodded and said, "*Ja, ja.*"

"It is good," the woman said. "It is pure, there is no ego, no filthy pride."

"Yes," I said.

"Can you send these garbages to Germany?" she asked.

"Yes," I said. "We ship our art worldwide."

"It is good," said the woman. She spoke again to the man in German, who once again answered, "*Ja, ja.*"

"And the price is?"

I handed her one of the price lists that sat on the counter, and pointed to the price of each piece; they were all untitled, numbered, and priced at $16,000.

The woman looked at it and then showed it to her companion, pointing to the price with a highly developed nail lacquered red.

"They are all available?" she asked.

I said they were.

"Not one has been sold?" she asked.

"There has been much interest," I said. "We are holding some. But no sales yet. Is there a particular one you are interested in?"

"The number 5 is very nice, we think."

"Ah, yes," I said, "that's my favorite."

"It is the best, you think?"

"Yes. I believe it is the artist's favorite, too."

"It is good," said woman. "Very good. We may return here. You have a card for us?"

I handed them one of the gallery's cards. "Would you like to join our mailing list?" I asked, indicating the guest book.

"Ja," she said. "Of course. Although probably we are already there."

She signed the book, and handed the pen back to me. It was a Waterman fountain pen; my mother thought it was very classy to have such a pen, but of course people were always trying to walk out with it, so it made things very difficult. Whenever anyone signed the book I had to watch them and make sure I got the pen back. I thought the resultant asking for the pen back pretty much countered any classy aspect it provided, but my mother was undeterred.

Later that afternoon, when I returned to the gallery with John's snack, my mother was standing at the front desk, going through her bag. My mother spends much of her life going through her bag. She always carries around these huge bags in which she stows everything and can never find anything.

"My sunglasses have disappeared," she announced. "As soon as I find them, I'm leaving. Do you want to walk home with me?"

"It's only four o'clock," I said.

"Yes, and it's a Friday afternoon in July. Anyone who is even remotely interested in art has already left the borough. Is that for John? Tell him he can leave, too."

I brought the frothy and expensive beverage in to John. "She says you can leave," I said. I could tell by the intent way he was looking at his computer screen he was gent4genting.

"Great," he said. "I'll be right behind you. Just finishing up some work."

"Have a good weekend," I said.

"You too."

My mother had miraculously found her sunglasses and we left the gallery and walked down the hall and waited for the freight elevator, which is the only elevator in the building and is operated by friendly men who relish their ability to dawdle and delay gallery folk.

Out on the street we turned west and walked the one block to the West Side Highway. We waited for the light to change and then walked over to the Hudson River promenade, which was, at this hour, teeming with Rollerbladers, bicyclists, and joggers: a sort of mobile, healthy happy hour.

It was nice, though, walking along the river. We passed a cart selling frozen lemonades and my mother bought us each one. "Did you have lunch with your father today?" she asked me.

"Yes," I said.

"Did you tell him about me?"

"Yes."

"I wish you wouldn't do that, James. He doesn't need to know every little thing that happens in my life."

"I don't think that's a little thing," I said.

"You know what I mean," she said. "Where did he take you?"

"The partners' dining room."

"My God, you can't even get a decent lunch out of that man. Do they let women in there yet?"

"I guess," I said. "As long as they're partners."

"Which, of course, they are not," said my mother. "What did you have?"

Like so many people who eat the majority of their meals in restaurants, my mother is always curious about what other people ordered other places. "Penne," I said. "With fresh basil and heirloom tomatoes."

"Was it good?"

"Yes," I said. I thought about telling her what my father had said about pasta, but I decided to skip it.

"I had lunch at Florent with Frances Sharpe. Did you know her daughter goes to Brown?"

"No," I said.

"Yes," said my mother. "Olivia Dark-Sharpe. She's going to be a junior. Unfortunately she's spending her junior year in Honduras. Apparently Brown has some program there, where you teach crafts to the natives."

"Shouldn't it be the other way around?"

"What do you mean?" my mother asked.

"Why do Honduran people need Brown students to teach them how to make crafts?"

"Frances explained it to me. Apparently the crafts they make are no good. So this program gets them making crafts that can be sold abroad, like tote bags and scented candles and soaps."

"Well, I can't wait for my junior year."

"Don't be smart, James. Frances says Olivia adores Brown."

"Adores?"

"Yes: adores. What's wrong with that?"

"I don't know. I just think it's a little weird to adore a college."

"Sometimes I can't stand you, James. You're so reluctant to show any enthusiasm about anything, or even allow it in other people. It's very annoying, and immature."

"That's not true," I said. "I'm enthusiastic about many things."

"Such as?"

"Well, that house I showed you last night, for instance."

"What house?"

"The house in Kansas. With the sleeping porch."

"Well, since that has absolutely no bearing on your life, it hardly counts. What in your life are you enthusiastic about? What do you adore?"

"I adore Trollope," I said. "And Denton Welch and Eric Rohmer."

"Who's Denton Welch?"

"A brilliant writer. He was British, and he wanted to be a painter, but when he was eighteen or something he got run over by a car while bicycling and became a permanent invalid who couldn't paint, so he began writing."

"That sounds morbid. Although I do admire people who make the best of adversities."

"He was an amazing writer. You shouldn't make fun of him."

"I'm not," said my mother. "But, James, those are all cultural things—books and films—it's easy to like them. It's easy to like art. It's liking life that's important. Anyone can like the Sistine Chapel."

"I hate the Sistine Chapel," I said. "I hate that Michelangelo had to waste his talent pandering to the Roman Catholic Church."

"Well, fine—hate the Sistine Chapel. But like something real."

"You don't think books are real?"

"You know what I mean—something that isn't created. Something that exists."

"I would like the old Penn Station, but it doesn't exist anymore."

"Well, what about Grand Central? Grand Central Station is wonderful, and thanks to Jacqueline Kennedy Onassis, it still exists."

"Well, I do like Grand Central. But you can't live there."

"Of course you can't live there! What, you won't be happy unless you live in Grand Central Station? That doesn't bode well, my dear."

I didn't answer. I knew my mother was right, but that didn't change the way I felt about things. People always think that if they can prove they're right, you'll change your mind.

We walked for a while in silence and then my mother said, "What's new with your father?"

I thought about telling her about my father's elective cosmetic surgery, which would have delighted her, but decided not to. The only way my parents ever find things out about each other is through Gillian and me, but since my mother had scolded me for disclosing her marriage debacle, I saw no reason to cooperate. So I said, "Nothing."

"Are you going out to East Hampton this weekend?" she asked.

"I don't think so," I said. "I think I'll go see Nanette tomorrow."

Nanette is my grandmother: my mother's mother. She lives in Hartsdale and she's probably my favorite person. She's called Nanette because she thinks it sounds more sophisticated than Grandma or Nana, and plus she understudied the star (I think it was Debbie Reynolds, but I'm not sure) in some revival of *No, No, Nanette* in the seventies. For many years she was a panelist on a TV game show called *You Don't Say.* She got to wear a different dress every day, all provided by some department store. She often refers to herself as "the poor man's Kitty Carlisle Hart."

"Do me a favor," my mother continued. "Don't tell Nanette about Barry and me. She'll find out soon enough and I'd like a few days of peace and quiet before she begins haranguing me."

"What if she asks me?"

"What if she asks you what?"

"About you and Mr. Rogers?"

"She won't ask. You know she never asks about me. She doesn't even think about me."

"Well, if she does ask, what should I say? Do you want me to lie?"

"Believe me, James," my mother said. "She won't ask."

◆ ◆ ◆

Later that night I was sitting on the couch in the living room with Miró trying to complete the *New York Times* crossword puzzle that my mother had left three-quarters finished, but since it was Friday and basically impossible I wasn't making much progress. My mother had gone to bed. About eleven o'clock Gillian and Herr Schultz came in from seeing some stupid movie. I don't understand how supposedly intelligent people— say a professor at Columbia University and a student at Barnard College—can go see a movie like *Pirates of the Caribbean*. Gillian went into the kitchen and came out with a bottle of Peroni beer for her and a diet, caffeine-free Coke for Rainer Maria. "Do you want a beer?" Gillian asked, but she waited until she had come into the room and sat down before asking this question, which implied I should say no.

I did (say no).

"How was the movie?" I asked.

"It was great," said Gillian. "At least the part we saw. But somebody started a fire in the theater, so we had to leave. They gave us free passes."

"I don't know why you would go see a movie like that on Friday night in New York," I said. "It's like going to hell."

"Get a life, James," said Gillian.

"Children, don't bicker," said Herr Schultz. "I get enough of that at home." Rainer Maria was married and had several alarmingly blond children. His wife, Kirsten, taught Scandinavian languages at Columbia (I'm sure there was huge demand for that) and wrote a series of mystery novels featuring a Swedish transsexual detective (female → male). Kirsten was having an affair with her former therapist. She and Rainer Maria had an "open" marriage. (I know all this because Gillian told me.)

"Guess what?" I said to Gillian.

"What?" she said.

"Dad's having plastic surgery this weekend."

"Cool. What's he getting done?"

"He's having the bags under his eyes removed."

"It's about time," said Gillian. "He's beginning to look like Walter Matthau. So that means he won't be at the house this weekend?"

"Yes," I said.

She turned to Rainer Maria. "Do you want to go to the beach tomorrow, sweetie?"

"No," he said. "I hate the beach. And please don't call me sweetie."

"Are you going out there?" Gillian asked me.

"No," I said. "I'm going to see Nanette tomorrow."

"You're so weird."

"Fuck you," I said.

"Children, children," said Rainer Maria.

"Well, don't you think it's weird?" Gillian asked Rainer Maria. "An eighteen-year-old boy who visits his grandmother?"

"No," said Rainer Maria. "You Americans have so little family feeling. In Germany, it is different. We love our grandparents."

"I'm not saying you shouldn't love them," said Gillian. "I just think visiting them is weird. It will be so good for you to go away to school, James. You really have to get out of this house."

"I've decided I'm not going to college," I said.

"What? Since when?"

"Today."

"What do you mean, you're not going to college? What are you going to do?"

"I'm thinking about moving to the Midwest."

"The Midwest? The Midwest of what?"

"The United States," I said. "The prairie states."

"The *prairie* states? I think you've read *My Ántonia* one too many times."

"Hush, Gillian. I think this is a very good plan for you, James," said Rainer Maria. "The college experience in the United States is a farce."

"Hello!" said Gillian. "You teach in a college."

"My dear Gillian, if everyone had to believe in the work he did, not much would get done in the world," said Rainer Maria.

"Have you told Mom about this?"

"I mentioned it to her."

"What do you mean, mentioned it? How can you mention you're not going to college a month before you're set to go?"

"I mentioned it. I think she thought I was joking."

"I'm sure she did. What's wrong with you? Why don't you want to go to college?"

"I think it would be a waste of time, and I wouldn't like the people. I don't want to live with people like that."

"Like what?"

"Like you."

"I think you make a lot of sense, James," said Rainer Maria.

Gillian hit him. "What do you mean? He just said he didn't want to live with people like me."

"I mean about it being a waste of time, and I don't think James would like the people, and that's no reflection on you, my dear."

Gillian finished her beer and stood up. "I'm hungry," she said. "Let's go get something to eat."

"All right," said Rainer Maria. "But someplace quiet. And cheap."

"Let's go to Primo."

"Primo is neither quiet nor cheap," said R.M.

I stood up. "I'm going to bed."

"Yes, you better rest up," said Gillian. "You have a big day tomorrow."

"Will you take Miró out?"

"No," said Gillian. "I walked him twice today, and he pooped both times."

"I will walk the dog!" said Rainer Maria. "When I return, you will have thought of an appropriate restaurant, Gillian. Good night, James."

"Good night, Rainer Maria." I did not say good night to Gillian, and she did not say good night to me.

5

May 2003

For a few weeks after my disastrous return from The American Classroom, very little was said about the incident. Because the police had been involved, my school was notified, and my guidance counselor, a woman with the unfortunate name of Ms. Kuntz (pronounced "Koontz") called me into her office and asked me if I wanted to talk about what had happened. I of course said no, which I could tell relieved her, and she said that since The American Classroom was an extracurricular activity not associated with the school, she saw no reason why the information should be included in my transcript or passed on to Brown. "We'll just pretend the whole thing never happened," she told me, and I said that was fine with me.

For a while it appeared as though my parents were going to take the same tactic, for neither of them mentioned it, but I knew they were probably just deciding how to deal with it. Ever since my parents divorced there has been this delayed response to Gillian's and my transgressions, for they must get together and agree on what to do, and since they don't like to get together and rarely agree, time invariably passes.

And then one night in May, my mother came into my bedroom and said, "I want to talk to you."

I was sitting at my computer and I said, "So talk."

"No," she said. "Shut that off. Or at least turn around and look at me."

I swiveled around so I was facing her. She was sitting on my bed. She looked at me appraisingly for a moment as if I might be an impostor, and then said, "I had lunch with your father today."

I said nothing. I wasn't quite sure where this was going, but I couldn't imagine it going anywhere pleasant, so I saw no point in advancing the conversation.

My mother waited a moment and then said, "We had a little talk about you."

"Little?" I said. "A chat perhaps? A tête-à-tête?"

"I am just going to ignore your tiresome remarks, James. We had a little talk about you."

"What is there to talk about me?"

"What is there not to talk about would be the better question. We are both worried about you. We talked about that."

"Why are you worried about me?"

"Why are we worried? James, you don't have any friends, you rarely speak, you apparently had some sort of psychotic episode at The American Classroom that caused you to act both irresponsibly and dangerously. That is what worries us."

"Well, as long as I'm happy, why should you worry?"

My mother leaned toward me. "Are you happy? Are you happy, James?" She asked these questions almost fiercely, with a disturbing vehement anguish. It scared me. I realized she was worried. Because my parents have often acted so irresponsibly, I forget that they do feel responsible for me and Gillian. Perhaps because they see their divorce as failing us in some way (which of course it did), they feel even more responsible, but I think it is a Sisyphean task, the thought of which both exhausts and immobilizes them, and so they avoid it as long as possible, and then at the last moment switch into this alarming über-parent mode. My mother was all buggy-eyed and a vein in her temple throbbed.

"No," I said, after a moment. "I'm not happy."

"That is why we are worried about you," my mother said gently. "We are worried because you are not happy. We want you to be happy." She sat back.

"Well, who's happy?" I said. "I don't think anyone is happy. How can anyone be happy in the world we—"

"Stop it, James," my mother said. "People are happy. Sometimes. Or they are not unhappy in the way that you are unhappy."

"In what way am I unhappy?" I asked.

"In a way that concerns us," said my mother. "A way that frightens us."

"Oh," I said. I couldn't really think of what to say.

"And so we had lunch," my mother continued, her voice

sounding a bit more normal. "And we had a talk about you. And we thought that perhaps you might like to talk to someone."

"Talk to someone? You just mentioned my disinclination to talk. Why would I want to talk to someone?"

"I don't mean *someone* someone," my mother said. "I mean someone a doctor. A therapist. A psychiatrist. A someone like that. Will you do this, James? For me? And your father. Just— just stop rejecting everything for a moment and go and talk to this woman."

"She's a woman?"

"Yes, she's a woman."

"Who picked her?"

"Your father did. I knew you would reject out of hand anybody I suggested."

"Well, you have to admit your record with therapists isn't very good."

My mother said nothing.

"What's her name?"

"Rowena Adler," my mother said. "Dr. Rowena Adler. She's a psychiatrist."

"Rowena? You're sending me to a shrink named Rowena?"

"What's wrong with Rowena? It's a perfectly fine name."

"I suppose if you're a character in a Wagnerian opera. But don't you think it's a tad Teutonic?"

"You're being ridiculous, James. You cannot reject this doctor because of her heritage. Your father talked to several people and she is apparently very good."

"Well, that's reassuring. A shrink vetted by Dad's insane colleagues."

"Your father has connections. He can find the best divorce lawyer, so why shouldn't he be able to find the best shrink? He put a lot of time and effort into this, and you know how unlike him that is. Dr. Adler comes highly recommended by people who know about these things. In fact, her specialty is . . ."

"What? What's her specialty? Silent, unhappy eighteen-year-olds?"

"Yes," said my mother. "In fact that is precisely her specialty. She works with disturbed adolescents."

"Oh, so that's what I am? It doesn't sound very PC. Can't they come up with something better? Can't I be a special adolescent? Or a differently abled adolescent? Can't—"

My mother reached out and put her hand over my mouth. "Stop," she said. "Just stop."

Her hand felt odd against my face. It felt weirdly intimate—I couldn't remember when she had last touched me. She kept her hand there, covering my mouth, for a long moment. And then she took it away. "I'm sorry," she said. "I shouldn't have—it's just that—"

"No," I said. "You're right. It's true."

"What's true?" my mother asked.

"I am disturbed," I said. I thought about what the word meant, what it really means to be disturbed, like how a pond is disturbed when you throw a rock into it or how you disturb the peace. Or how you can be disturbed by a book or movie or the burning rain forest or the melting ice caps. Or the war in Iraq. It

was one of those moments when you feel you have never heard
the word before, and you cannot believe it means what it means,
and you think how did this word come to mean that? It seemed
like a bell or something, shining and pure, *disturbed, disturbed, disturbed*, I could hear it pealing with its true meaning, and I said, as
if I had just realized it, "I am disturbed."

I was disappointed with Rowena Adler's office. I had imagined it
would be in a Village brownstone, facing the garden perhaps,
with Danish modern furniture and kilims on the parquet floor
and tasteful abstract paintings on the walls, and she would sit in
a big swively chair and I would sit across from her, or perhaps recline on a divan at her side, and maybe she would have a dog or a
cat, an old dog or cat, quiet and tired, who slept at her feet, but I
first met her in an office in a New York University Medical Center building on a godforsaken stretch of First Avenue. I had to
wait in a windowless room lined with the rows of interconnected
molded plastic seats you often see in bus terminals. There was
also a watercooler, but it was empty. There is something inher-
ently depressing about an empty watercooler—none of that is it
half-full or half-empty, just empty—and I thought if I were a
shrink and had a watercooler in my waiting room I would make
sure it was always filled. This room obviously served as the waiting room for several other health practitioners, and I was a little
alarmed to think that Dr. Adler couldn't afford her own office,
with a private entrance and a private waiting room. This was like
going to the dentist, if you went to a dentist in a public health
clinic in the Port Authority Bus Terminal.

A woman sat across from me eating a grossly overstuffed tuna salad sandwich. There was so much tuna salad in this woman's sandwich that it was oozing out of the roll onto the waxed paper she had spread on her lap, and she reached down and picked up clumps of it with her fingers and fed them to herself. I could tell she was trying to do this daintily, but of course the inherent piggishness of the activity made that impossible.

A woman appeared in the doorway. Although there was only me and the tuna sandwich lady, she looked around the room as if it were full of people and said, "James? James Sveck?"

"Yes," I said. I stood up and approached her.

She held out her hand and I shook it. It felt very cool and slender. "I'm Dr. Adler," she said. "Why don't you come with me?"

I followed her down a depressing hallway into a tiny windowless office that might have housed an accountant. In fact it reminded me a bit of Myron Axel's closet, filled with piles of paper waiting to be filed, week-old cups of coffee turned into science experiments, and a litter of broken umbrellas nesting beneath the desk.

I must have looked as surprised as I felt when I entered her office, for Rowena Adler looked at the utilitarian clutter about her and said, "I'm sorry about this mess. I'm so used to it. I forget how it looks." Then she sat down and said, "It's nice to meet you, James."

I said, "Thank you," as if she had paid me a compliment. I wasn't about to say it was nice to meet her, too. I hate saying anything expected like that, that kind of dead, meaningless language.

"Why don't you sit down there," she said, indicating an

uncomfortable-looking metal folding chair. It was the only other chair in the room, but she said it as if there were many and she had selected this one especially for me. She was sitting in a tweed-covered office chair on casters that was turned away from her desk. The room was so small our knees almost touched. She leaned back, ostensibly to be more comfortable, but I could tell it was really to move away from me. "I usually see patients in my office downtown, but on Thursdays I can't get away from here, and I wanted to see you as soon as I could."

I didn't like the way she called me a patient, or implied I was a patient, although since she was a doctor and I was consulting her I'm not sure what else I could be. A client sounded too businesslike, but she could have just said "people," but then I thought I was wrong to be offended: there is nothing shameful about being a patient, one does not bring sickness upon oneself, it is an unelected characteristic—cancer and tuberculosis are not indications of people's character (I had read Susan Sontag's *Illness as Metaphor* in my modern morals class last spring), but then I thought, Well, maybe with psychiatry it's different, because if you're manic-depressive or paranoid or sexually compulsive it is rather indicative of your character, or at least inextricably linked with your character, and these things must be bad, otherwise they would not be treated, so being a patient in these circumstances *was* an indication of some sort of personal failure or—

"So, James," I suddenly heard her saying, "what brings you here?"

This seemed a stupid question to me. If you go to a dentist you can say "I have a toothache," or you go into a jeweler's and

ask to have a new battery installed in your watch, but what could
you possibly say to a psychiatrist?

"What brings me here?" I repeated the question, hoping she
would rephrase it more intelligibly.

"Yes." She smiled, pointedly ignoring my tone. "What brings
you here?"

"I suppose if I knew what brought me here, I wouldn't be
here," I said.

"Where would you be?"

"I'm afraid I don't know," I said.

"You're afraid?"

I realized that she was one of those annoying people who
take everything you say literally. "I misspoke," I said. "I'm not
afraid. I just don't know."

"Are you sure?"

"Sure of what? That I don't know or that I'm not afraid?"

"Which do you think I mean?"

"Please don't do that," I said.

"Please don't do what?"

I thought that at the rate we were repeating each other's
words we wouldn't get very far in forty-five minutes. "Please don't
answer a question with a question in that therapy way."

Without any reaction or hesitation she said, "What do you
think about therapy?"

I felt like we were in some contest to see who could unnerve
the other first. This did not seem very therapeutic to me, but I
was intent upon winning. "I think therapy is a rather misguided
notion of capitalist societies whereby the self-indulgent examina-

tion of one's life supersedes the actual living of said life." I had no idea where this came from—perhaps I had read it or heard it in a movie?

"Sad life?" she said.

"No. Said life."

"Oh, I thought you said 'sad.' "

"No, I said 'said.' "

"I was just saying I misunderstood what you said. I didn't mean to imply you hadn't said it."

"Well, I'm glad that's been cleared up," I said.

She peered at me intently for a moment, and then said, "So why are you here?"

"Isn't that just another way of asking what brought me here?"

"Yes," she said. She just barely smiled.

"But I told you I don't know what brought me here."

"So you don't know why you're here?"

"It would follow," I said.

"You have absolutely no idea, in any sense, why you are here?"

"I'm here because my parents wanted me to come here."

"So you do know why you're here?" she asked.

I didn't say anything. It just seemed pointless, like trying to have a conversation with a parrot or someone who's been lobotomized. And then I wondered if Dr. Adler might perform lobotomies. She was, after all, a medical doctor. But I supposed brain surgeons, not psychiatrists, performed lobotomies. If they are still performed. I'm fascinated with the idea of lobotomies, the idea of opening up the brain and snipping around a bit and then closing it up again, like fixing a car or something. And the person wakes up and is a little stupid but stupid in a happy, untroubled way. I'm also fascinated by shock therapy—all these things that are done to alter people's brains. When we were young, Gillian and I used to play a game called Mental Asylum. Gillian was the doctor and I was the patient and she would administer shock treatment to me. She'd anoint my temples with a cotton ball dabbed with Listerine, shove her field hockey mouth guard into my mouth, and then clamp the stereo headphones on me. When she plugged the cord into the stereo I would go stiff and cross my eyes and tremble epileptically and Gillian would hold me down and say "ZZZZZZZZZZZZZZZZZZZ." It's odd what facets of life children incorporate into their play. I started to think about this, about how we wanted to assume the dreariest aspects of adult life: playing office, playing store, playing mental asylum, when I once again became aware that Dr. Adler was saying something.

"What?" I asked.

"Our time is up," she said. "I'll see—how about Tuesday? Are you free on Tuesdays?"

"Yes," I said.

"Fine. We'll meet at the same time, but at my downtown office. Here's the address." She handed me a business card.

I was trying to figure out how our session could be over so quickly. I wanted to look at my watch, but I couldn't bring myself to do this in front of her. I could tell she was acting all normal, as if all psychiatric sessions lasted ten minutes and most of the time was spent repeating each other or in silence.

"Does that work for you?" she asked.

"Yes," I said.

"Fine," she said. "See you then." She smiled brightly at me, as if we had had a very pleasant chat, and then swiveled around in her chair, turning her back on me in a way that was clearly dismissive.

6

Saturday, July 26, 2003

I took the 10:23 Harlem line train from Grand Central, which arrived in Hartsdale at 11:03. It was about a twenty-minute walk to my grandmother's house at 16 Wyncote Lane. She lives in a Tudor-style house that was built in the 1920s and miraculously still has all of its original Arts and Crafts features. No one's torn out the mahogany wainscoting or carpeted the mosaic tile floors or put aluminum siding over the brick and stucco and stone façade. The house is not air-conditioned, but because it is surrounded by very old shade trees and has thick stone walls, it stays fairly cool. What I like best about it is that every doorway in the house is rounded at the top, and every door is correspondingly shaped, beautiful paneled wooden doors that fit perfectly into their arched lintels. You get this nice (and rare) feeling that whoever built the house loved building it, and was not in a hurry.

When I arrived the front door was open and I peered through the screen door. The house looked dark and cool and quiet; there was a vase of dahlias on the table in the front hall, next to a stack of three library books. I leaned my face closer and called Nanette! through the screen. After a moment I heard her coming down the stairs, and then I could see her: first her feet, then her legs, and then the rest of her slowly appeared. My grandmother always walks down stairs slowly, turned sideways, leading with her hip, with one hand on the banister and her feet placed horizontally on the treads. She says a lady should never proceed down a staircase facing forward unless she wants to look like a charging bull. My grandmother is a firm believer in proper deportment; it is the closest she comes to any sort of religion.

"James," she said when she'd reached the bottom (another thing she believes is that it's impolite to talk when you're going up or down stairs). "I had a feeling I'd see you today. I woke up this morning and the first thing I thought was, I wouldn't be at all surprised if James comes visiting today." She opened the door. "Come in but be careful on this floor. I just washed it, so it may be slippery."

I stepped into the front hall. "What are you doing washing floors on Saturday morning?"

"It's just as good as any other day. Isn't it funny I knew you would come? I must be clairvoyant."

"Well, I did mention to you Wednesday that I might come visit you today," I said.

"Did you? Really? I don't remember that at all. Well, so much for my clairvoyance. Next time that happens, though, be a lamb and don't tell me. Humor an old lady. Do you want some juice or some coffee? Or some eggs and bacon? Have you had breakfast?"

"Yes," I said, "but some coffee would be nice."

"Well, let me brew a fresh pot, then." She walked down the hallway into her kitchen which was spotless, the pink Formica countertops bare except for her FLOUR SUGAR COFFEE tin canisters. Everything is always in its place in my grandmother's kitchen, including the things in the refrigerator and cupboards. She has one of those old refrigerators with only one door that you pull open with a crank.

"Sit down," she said. "The paper is there if you're interested." She opened the coffee tin and began to make coffee. I looked through the paper, which, being Saturday's, was rather thin. I did notice, however, that my grandmother had finished the crossword puzzle, which even my mother can rarely do on Saturdays. (It gets progressively more difficult throughout the week.)

My grandmother turned around as she filled the percolator at the sink. "When does your mother come home?"

"She's already home," I said.

"I thought they were going for a week."

"They were. But she came home early. On Thursday."

"Well, that shows good sense. Has Mr. Rogers moved in with you yet?"

Mr. Rogers had, in fact, moved in with us about two months ago, when my mother agreed to marry him, which was about six months after she met him. Fortunately he had not yet sold his apartment; he was waiting for the market to "pick up."

"Yes, he's moved in," I said. I couldn't believe I had honestly answered this many questions and still not divulged the real news.

"Well, I feel sorry for you, James," my grandmother said. "I wouldn't want to live in a house with that man. But then you'll be out of there soon enough, won't you?"

Instead of answering her question, I said, "What's your opinion of college?"

"Which college? Brown?"

"No—college in general."

"Well, I really don't have much of one, seeing as how I haven't been in college for—let me think—sixty years. No, what am I saying; I'm eighty-one—so fifty-seven."

"But are you glad you went to college? Was it a good experience?"

"I suppose it was. Although I can't remember a single thing I learned. Except for Latin, and that's only because the nuns literally beat it into us and I use it sometimes for the crossword."

"There were nuns at Radcliffe?"

"Yes, it was all nuns."

"Are you sure? At Radcliffe?"

"Maybe it was high school."

"But you aren't Catholic," I said. "I don't think you ever went to a parochial school."

"Well, I distinctly remember nuns with sticks walking up and down the aisles as we recited Latin. Maybe it was a show I was in, but I doubt it because nuns don't beat children in musicals."

I felt we were getting off the track, which often happens with my grandmother, so I said, "But did you think your four years at Radcliffe were valuable?"

"Well, if I hadn't gone to Radcliffe I wouldn't have met your grandfather, and that would have been a shame. And I wouldn't have gone into show business because you see my parents forbad me to perform in public until I got a master's degree, thinking I was too stupid or too lazy to get a master's degree. So yes, I suppose going to college was a good thing for me."

"I didn't know you had a master's degree."

"Oh yes," my grandmother said.

"What's it in?"

"Oh, I forget," she said. "Something harmless like sociology. Or maybe anthropology."

"Did you make good friends there?"

"Goodness, no. Only serious girls went to Radcliffe back then. Serious, booky girls with glasses and woolen stockings. A very unappealing bunch. I always wished I'd gone to Sweet Briar College like my sister Geraldine. The girls there were gay and lovely and never seemed to look at a book. They could keep their horses in the dormitory. But, James, this is all so long ago. Colleges are very different now. You should ask Gillian about this, not me."

My grandmother took two cups and two saucers out of the cabinet and put them on the kitchen table and then got the milk out of the refrigerator and poured it into a creamer and then unplugged the coffeepot and poured coffee into each cup. She returned the coffeepot to the counter and plugged it back in and then opened a drawer and found two small linen napkins, which she brought over to the table. She asked me if I wanted a cookie and I said no and then she sat down.

She put milk in her coffee and stirred it and pushed the creamer and sugar toward me and then said, "What's this all about? Are you thinking of not going to college, James?"

"Yes," I said. "How did you know?"

"Perhaps I am clairvoyant after all," she said.

"Well, do you think I should go to college?"

"I suppose I'd have to know what you would do if you didn't, but I hardly see why what I thought would be of any interest to you."

"Well, I am interested. I wouldn't ask you if I weren't."

"Why don't you want to go to college?"

She was the third person who had asked me that question in as many days, and I felt I was getting worse instead of better at answering it. My grandmother waited patiently for my answer. She pretended there were crumbs on the table that needed brushing off.

After a moment I said, "It's hard for me to explain why I don't want to go. All I can say is there's nothing about going that appeals to me. I don't want to be in that kind of social environment, I've been with people my own age all my life and I don't really like them or seem to have much in common with them, and I feel that anything I want to know I can learn from reading books—basically that's what you do in college anyway—and I feel I can do that on my own and not waste all that money on something I don't think I need or want. I think I could do other things with the money that would be better for me than going to college."

"Such as?" my grandmother asked.

I didn't answer because it was suddenly clear to me, for a second or two, that part of this not wanting to go to college was simply a desire not to move forward, for I loved where I was at the moment, and felt that so surely and keenly: sitting there, in my grandmother's kitchen, drinking her freshly percolated coffee from coffee cups and not from cardboard cups with sippy lids, sitting in her perfectly ordered kitchen with the back door open so a bit of a breeze moved through the house, and the electric clock above the sink humming quietly all night and all day, and the linoleum floor worn down from so many years of washing and scrubbing it was as smooth as leather, and my grandmother sitting across from me in her dress she had probably bought forty years ago and worn a thousand times since then, listening to me, seeming to accept me in a way that no one else did, and the safe summer Saturday occurring outside, all around us, the world not yet totally violated by stupidity and intolerance and hate.

"What is it you'd like to do?" my grandmother asked.

"I'd like to buy a house," I said. "A nice house, in some small town in the Midwest, a house like this house, an old house, with things like this—" and I reached out and touched the small metal door that opened into a sort of safe built into the wall that had a matching door outside, where the milkman (when there were still milkmen) would deposit glass bottles of milk or cream and take away the empty bottles, so early in the morning the fresh milk would be there, waiting in the walls of your house.

"And what would you do in this house?"

"I would read. I would read a lot, all the books I've wanted to read but haven't been able to because of school, and find some job, like working in a library or as a night watchman or something like that, and I'd learn a craft, like bookbinding or weaving or carpentry, and make things, nice things, and take care of the house and the garden and the yard." I found the idea of being a librarian very appealing—working in a place where people had to whisper and only speak when necessary. If only the world were like that!

"But wouldn't you be lonely? Moving so far away? Living amongst strangers?"

"I don't mind being lonely," I said. "I am lonely now, here, living in New York. It makes it worse in New York because you see people interacting everywhere you go, all the time. Constantly."

"Just because people interact doesn't mean they aren't lonely."

"I know," I said.

"If I were you, I'd take the money and travel. Go to Mexico. Go to Europe. Go to Timbuktu."

"I don't believe in traveling. I don't think it's natural. I think it's too easy to travel now. I don't want to go anywhere I can't walk to."

"So you're going to walk to Kansas?"

"I would like to. I think the only way to really know where you are is to walk there. Or at least stay on the ground—drive or take a train. But I think walking is the best. It gives you a true sense of distance."

"I don't understand you, James. You're so intent on making your life impossible. It doesn't bode well. Life is difficult enough, you know."

"I know," I said. "But I'm not . . . just because I don't want to go to college, or don't want to go to Mexico, doesn't mean I'm making my life impossible."

"Well, you certainly aren't making it easy." My grandmother stood and took her empty cup of coffee to the sink. She rinsed the cup and saucer under the faucet and then dried them with the dish towel that hung from the refrigerator's upraised arm. Then she put them carefully back in the cupboard, in the spaces allotted them. "Would you like more coffee?" she asked.

"No, thank you," I said.

She unplugged the percolator and poured the hot coffee down the sink. Then she rinsed the sink and scoured it with a sponge and Comet.

"Do you really think I'm making my life impossible?" I asked her. "Do you think I should forget all this and just go to college?"

She put the sponge down and wiped her damp hands with the dish towel. She turned to me and looked at me for a moment. It was a hard look. I felt I had failed her, or disappointed her, in some way. Or that I had broken a rule of decorum I did not know existed.

My grandmother hung the towel back up and said, "Let's forget about the future for the nonce—it's so dispiriting. It's almost lunchtime, let's think about that. How do you feel about egg salad?"

I've always liked my grandmother's egg salad. She adds chopped-up bread-and-butter pickles. Everyone else seems to think it's disgusting, but we both like it.

"I feel good about egg salad," I said.

"Good," said my grandmother. "So do I."

7

May 2003

DR. ADLER'S DOWNTOWN OFFICE WAS A PLEASANTER PLACE than her space at the Medical Center, but it wasn't the sun-filled haven I had imagined. It was a rather small dark office in a suite of what I assumed were several small dark offices on the ground floor of an old apartment building on Tenth Street. In addition to her desk and chair there was a divan, another chair, a ficus tree, and some folkloric-looking weavings on the wall. And a bookcase of dreary books. I could tell they were all nonfiction because they all had titles divided by colons: *Blah Blah Blah: The Blah Blah Blah of Blah Blah Blah.* There was one window that probably faced an airshaft because the rattan shade was lowered in a way that suggested it was never raised. The walls were painted a pale yellow, in an obvious (but unsuccessful) attempt to "brighten up" the room.

Dr. Adler sat in her chair and indicated the other chair to

me, which was a relief because I wasn't about to lie on the couch. I've seen too many Woody Allen movies and *New Yorker* cartoons to do that.

She looked different this time: less harum-scarum, more elegant, almost soignée. She had her hair up and was wearing a sleeveless summer dress that revealed her rather muscular arms. She must play tennis, I thought. Or shot-put.

She crossed her legs and then joined her hands in her lap with her two forefingers raised together in a steeple. She smiled at me. "So," she said. "Here we are again."

I was going to correct her because we were not *here* again, we were meeting again, but as our first meeting had been in a different place, we could hardly be here *again*. But I knew if I said that we would start to spar with each other as we had at the previous session, and I wasn't in the mood for that. So I asked, "Why don't you have any novels?"

"What?" she asked.

I nodded at the bookcase, which was behind her. "I notice you don't have any fiction in your bookcase. I just wondered why."

She turned around and studied the books as if I might have been lying. Then she turned back to me. "Why do you ask?" she said.

"Do you have to ask me that? Can't you just answer the question?"

"This is my office," she said. "It's the place where I work. I keep the books associated with my work here."

"And novels aren't associated with your work?"

"You are free to conclude that."

I didn't say anything. I suddenly felt sad. I knew I was being belligerent, but I couldn't stop.

After a moment she said, "Actually, you're wrong. I do have fiction here." She swiveled around and bent to retrieve a volume from the bottom shelf, and then she swiveled back and showed it to me: it was an old Scribner's paperback edition of *The Age of Innocence*. "I keep this here to read," she said. "In case a patient doesn't show up, or is late."

I didn't know what to say. I felt somehow ashamed, and I still felt sad and hopeless.

Dr. Adler put the book down on the floor beside her chair, as if she wanted to keep it visible, almost include it in our session. Then she folded her hands in her lap and looked at me.

"Have you read Trollope?" I asked.

"I don't think so," she said. "Although I suppose I might have read something of his in college."

"What about Proust?"

"No, I have not read Proust. Is that a problem for you?"

"No," I said. "I just wondered. I haven't read Proust either. Someone told me not to read Proust until I had already fallen into and out of love." (Actually this was John Webster. I was planning on reading *Remembrance of Things Past*, or *In Search of Lost Time*, or *À la recherche du temps perdu* all summer, but the first day I brought *Swann's Way* into the gallery he took it away from me and said it was a crime to read Proust at my age. He made me promise I wouldn't read it until I had both found and lost love. I have to admit I was sort of relieved because I had found it hard going, but I had only read about thirty pages.)

"I see," she said.

I hate when people say "I see." It doesn't mean anything and I think it's hostile. Whenever anyone tells me "I see" I think they're really saying "Fuck you." I was going to ask her what she saw, but I realized that wouldn't get us anywhere, so I said nothing.

After a moment of silence she said, "How are you feeling today?"

I realized that being in a shrink's office and having the shrink ask me how I felt made me sad, so I said, "I feel sad." For some reason, I closed my eyes.

"Do you?" she asked.

"Yes," I said.

After a moment she asked, "Do you know why you feel sad?"

I opened my eyes. Although it had only been a few seconds, I felt as if I had been away a long time, although everything was the same. Dr. Adler watched me patiently, in the way a psychiatrist would watch a patient, her face perfectly devoid of any expression except for a slight smear of concern. After a moment she said, "How long have you felt this way?"

I know she meant generally but I couldn't say "forever." I couldn't say how many days or months or years. It wasn't like I woke up one morning and had a fever.

"For quite some time," I said.

"Days?" she asked. "Weeks? Months?" She paused. "Years?"

"Years," I said.

"I happen to know your parents are divorced. Do you think your sadness is connected to that?"

"Well, it certainly didn't help."

"So you were sad before then?"

"Yes," I said, "and I wish you would tell me what else you know about me. I assume you talked to my father."

"I did. Actually I spoke with both your parents. But only briefly."

"What did they tell you?"

"They told me they were worried because you didn't seem very happy. They told me you're antisocial and seem lonely. They also mentioned the incident with the National Classroom last month."

"It was The American Classroom," I said.

She made a what's-the-difference face.

"What did they say about that?"

"They said you had some problems dealing with a group dynamic and had an experience of panic."

"An experience of panic—is that what they called it?"

"Those are probably my words. Would you express it differently?"

"No," I said, "that just about sums it up."

"Is there anything you would add?"

"You mean are there other things wrong with me?"

"Did you think that was a list of things wrong with you?"

"You really can't stop it, can you?"

"Stop what?"

"Answering questions with questions. You sound exactly like a therapist."

"I *am* a therapist, James. A psychiatrist, in fact. A doctor. I'm not here to chat with you in ways you deem are appropriate. I think you know that."

I said nothing, in a way I hoped didn't seem sulky.

"Do you know that?" she asked.

"Yes," I said. "I know that. It's just that . . ."

"What?"

"When you do that, respond to me in that way, it seems so stupid to me. It's so predictable. I mean, I could do it. I know exactly what you're going to say. I could stay at home and have our conversation."

"Then why are you here? Why are you wasting your time? My time?"

"I don't know. I guess because my parents wanted me to come. This is their way of trying to help me, and I wanted to let them think that."

"Think what?"

"That they were helping me."

"So you don't think that this will help you?"

"I didn't say that."

"I know. But you implied it. At least I think you did. That's why I'm asking you."

I looked around her office. I know it sounds terrible, but I was discouraged by the ordinariness, the expectedness, of it. It was as if there was a catalog for therapists to order a complete of-

fice from: furniture, carpet, wall hangings, even the ficus tree
seemed depressingly generic. Like one of those little paper pellets
you put in water that puffs up and turns into a lotus blossom.
This was like a puffed-up shrink's office.

"How should I know if this will help me? It's like asking
someone who's swimming the English Channel if they will get
across. There's no way they can know."

"Yes, but they can *believe* they can swim across. Otherwise
why would they set out? You wouldn't begin to swim across the
Channel if you were sure you couldn't make it."

"You might," I said.

"Would you? Why?"

"I can't believe we're talking about people swimming across
the English Channel."

"It was an analogy that you made."

"I know. I just don't think it deserves this kind of scrutiny."

She sort of squinted for a moment, and then said, "Why do
you think you used that analogy?"

I shrugged. "I don't know," I said.

"Well, think about it," she said. "Why the English Channel?"

"Because I see not feeling sad as a sort of Herculean task."

"Yes, but any number of tasks might be considered Herculean. In fact, Hercules performed seven tasks. Why do you
think you chose swimming the English Channel?"

I was fairly certain that Hercules performed more than
seven tasks (I checked later and I was right: it was twelve), but I
decided to let that pass. "I don't know," I said. "It's sort of old-
fashioned. People don't really do it anymore. And I guess En-

gland and France seem so different to me, so totally different, like sadness and happiness."

"Which is sad and which is happy?"

I thought this was a particularly stupid question, but I decided not to resist anymore. It seemed easier to just go along with her. "Well, I suppose England is sad, but only because I think of people swimming from England to France and not vice versa. But the French do seem to be happier, or at least I imagine they are, what with the better food and weather and fashion."

"Is that what makes people happy: food and fashion and weather?"

"No," I said. "It's the other way around. Happy people make good food and fashion. If you're happy you don't want to eat potted meat or haggis. If you're happy you want to wear clothes that make you look beautiful, not sensible shoes and woolens. I guess one's mood doesn't affect the weather, but it might. It's possible."

Dr. Adler was quiet for a moment, and then said, "I'm surprised to hear that you don't like to talk."

I know she meant this as an encouraging observation and not an accusation, but something prevented me from responding accordingly. "Well, I don't," I said.

"I don't doubt you," she said. "I'm just surprised. You sound quite articulate to me, and it also seems as if you enjoy talking."

"Well, I don't," I said, and I could hear how ridiculously petulant I sounded.

"Why? What is it about talking that you don't like?"

"I don't know," I said. "I just don't enjoy it."

"Is there anyone you enjoy talking with?"

I thought immediately of my grandmother, and then I thought of John: I liked talking to him, or listening to him. "Yes," I said.

"Who?"

"My grandmother and the guy that runs my mother's gallery."

"And what is it about them that makes you feel that way?"

"I don't know," I said. "They're both smart, and funny. They don't say stupid or boring things. Or obvious things. Most of what people say seems so obvious to me. And then they repeat it about thirteen times."

"And what is it about them as listeners that makes you enjoy talking to them?"

"I just like them. I respect them. It seems worthwhile to talk to them. I don't feel that way about many people."

"I see," she said. "So if you met more people that you liked and respected, you would enjoy talking more?"

"You would be free to conclude that," I said.

"And you don't think you might meet people like that at college? You're going to Brown, correct?"

"Supposedly," I said.

"I don't understand. Don't you think you might meet interesting people you would respect at Brown?"

"No," I said. "I do not."

"Why do you think that? What do you base that assumption upon?"

"Because I don't like people my age very much. Especially

when they are gathered in large groups. Which is exactly what I believe college is all about."

"So you'd be opposed to going to any college?"

"Well, any college comprised of a large group of people my age."

"What is it about people your age you don't like?"

"I just don't like them. I find them boring."

"Boring?"

"Yes."

"Why do you find them boring? What do you base that judgment on?"

"It's not a judgment," I said. "It's just a fact. It's how I feel."

"So you think it's all right to feel something generally about a large segment of the population, a certain group of people, a race or a creed of people, and conclude it is a fact that they are that way?"

"I didn't say it was a fact that people my age are boring. I said it was a fact that I find them boring."

"And you're comfortable with that distinction?"

"Yes. It's not as if I want to gas them or lynch them. I just don't particularly want to go to college with them."

"I see," she said.

"I know I'm not supposed to comment on what you say, but I really wish you would stop saying 'I see.'"

"Why?"

I said nothing.

"Does it bother you that I see?"

"No," I said.

"Then why don't you like me to say it?"

"I don't know," I said. "I don't really think it means that you see. Or I guess it means that you see, but not only that. It means that you see, and you don't approve. It implies a judgment, I think—an unfavorable judgment."

"It's a very neutral statement," she said. "It implies no judgment whatsoever. Perhaps you're projecting a judgment upon me."

"Perhaps I am," I said. "But can something be very neutral? Isn't neutrality an absolute, like uniqueness?"

She was silent a moment, and then she said, "Why do you think it's so important for you to control how other people speak?"

I hate questions that presuppose an idea. People think they can get away with things by doing that. "I wasn't aware I did that," I said.

"Really?" she asked. "You have no awareness of that?"

"That is what I said," I said.

"I know it's what you said. I'm asking you if it's true."

"Do you think I would lie to you?"

"My question indicates that I do," she said.

I was a bit taken aback by the tone of her voice. "I suppose yes, I am aware of something like that. But I don't think I control how other people speak."

"What is it that you do?"

"I don't know," I said. "I just don't like it when language is misused. I think people should speak correctly and clearly. Accurately."

"Why do you think that's important to you?"

I didn't say anything, because I couldn't think of anything to say.

"Do you think that tendency encourages people to talk to you?"

The answer was obvious, so I refused to give it.

We sat there for a long moment, shrouded in a hostile, somewhat sad silence. Finally she said, "Well, our time is up. I'll see you back here at the same time on Thursday. Does that work for you?"

"I thought I was coming once a week."

"I think two sessions a week would be better," she said. "At least for now. Is that a problem for you?"

"Not logistically," I said.

"Is it a problem in any other way?"

"No," I said.

"Good," she said. "Then I'll see you on Thursday at four-thirty."

8

June 2003

My sessions with Dr. Adler often began in silence. Actually they often progressed in silence, for Dr. Adler quickly made it clear that she was primarily, if not exclusively, a reactive therapist: apparently her methodology did not condone the initial asking of questions. So unless I had something to say, which I often did not, we would spend much of our sessions sitting in our chairs facing each other. She would smile at me with her false, unvarying smile, trying to look open and accepting, I suppose, as if all I needed to spill my guts was a friendly face. My silence was, I admit, often a response to hers: I didn't see why the burden of speaking should always be mine. And so I would often remain silent even when I could think of something to say, because the idea of articulating whatever it was I thought seemed too expected of me, too cooperative, too responsive. There are people who are uncomfortable with a silence, who rush to fill it by saying anything, thinking that anything is better than nothing, but I am not one of those people. I am not at all disquieted by silence. And neither, apparently, was Dr. Adler.

One day our session began in this quiet (silent) way, but it was not wholly due to my recalcitrance—I just couldn't think of anything to say. Dr. Adler had instructed me to always say whatever I was thinking, but this was difficult for me, for the act of thinking and the act of articulating those thoughts were not synchronous to me, or even necessarily consecutive. I knew that I thought and spoke in the same language and that theoretically there should be no reason why I could not express my thoughts as they occurred or soon thereafter, but the language in which I thought and the language in which I spoke, though both English, often seemed divided by a gap that could not be simultaneously, or even retrospectively, bridged.

I've always been fascinated by the idea of simultaneous translation, like at the UN where everyone is wearing little transmitters in their ears and you know that somewhere behind the scenes the simultaneous translators are listening and transforming what is said from one language into another. I understand how such a process is possible, but to me it seems miraculous— the idea that words can be thrown up into the air in one language and alight in another as quickly as a ball is thrown into the air and caught. I think there is some sort of sieve in my mind that prohibits the rapid (let alone simultaneous) transference of my thoughts into speech. Like one of those mesh drain guards in a bathtub, there is something that prevents my thoughts from leaving my mind, and so they collect, like those nasty damp coils of hair stuck to the mesh, and have to be forcibly removed.

I was thinking about these notions of speech and thought, thinking how difficult it would be for me to articulate them—or not difficult, but wearisome, as if thinking them was enough and expressing them would be redundant or inferior, for everyone knows things are diminished by translation, it is always best to read a book in its original language (*À la recherche du temps perdu*). Translations are merely subjective approximations and that is how I feel about everything I say: it is not what I am thinking but merely the closest I can get to it using the faulty reductive constraints of language. And so I often think it is better to say nothing than to express myself inexactly. This is what I was thinking when I realized that Dr. Adler was speaking. "What?" I said.

"You seem preoccupied. What are you thinking?"

"Nothing," I said.

She made a face indicating how lame she thought that was.

"Sometimes I resent having to express my thoughts," I said. "I was thinking about that."

"And why is that?"

"I don't know. It's just that they're mine. People don't go around sharing their blood or whatever. I don't see why we should always be expected to share such intimate parts of ourselves."

"People give blood," she said.

"Yes, but not constantly. Just a little bit, like once a year."

"So you're saying you should only share your thoughts a little bit, once a year?"

"No," I said. "Of course I wasn't saying that. And if you honestly thought I was saying that, it only proves my point that talking is ridiculous because it's impossible to communicate precisely what you think."

"Do you really believe that?" Dr. Adler asked.

"Yes," I said. "I do."

She paused for a moment, as if she was considering this statement, and then she said, "Well, why don't you tell me about what happened in Washington?"

I was shocked. She had never asked me a specific question like that or expressed interest in any particular event in my life. "What?" I asked.

"I said, Why don't you tell me about what happened in Washington. I've realized we've never talked about it. I think it would be good if we did."

"I really don't want to talk about what happened in Washington," I said.

"Why?"

"I don't know. It's stupid. I was—I couldn't deal with it and I did something stupid. But it's over, it's in the past. I really don't want to talk about it."

"What did you do?"

"You don't know? My parents didn't tell you?"

"No," she said. "I wouldn't be asking you if I knew."

I didn't believe that for a moment.

"It was some sort of youth government seminar you attended?"

I could tell she was trying to trick me into talking about it by asking innocuous questions.

"Yes," I said.

"Tell me about it," she said.

"It was this stupid supposedly nonpartisan program that brings two supposedly intelligent students from each state to Washington, D.C., for a week so they can be indoctrinated in how wonderful the American government is."

"And so your problem had to do with the nature of the program?"

"Well, no. I mean, that was certainly a problem, but I could deal with that."

"Yes, I think you'd be rather resistant to indoctrination."

I chose not to respond to this blatant attempt at flattery, but Dr. Adler was not deterred. "So what was it, then?" she asked. "What was the problem?"

"That question presupposes many things," I said.

She said nothing but made a motion with her hand, encouraging me to enumerate.

"It presupposes there was a 'problem.' It presupposes that I know what the problem was. It presupposes I know how to articulate the problem. It presupposes that I want, or am willing, to articulate the problem."

"I wouldn't argue with any of that," said Dr. Adler. "But the question itself remains."

"I hate this idea," I said. "This idea that there's a problem,

that there is something as simple as a problem, and you can iden-
tify the problem, and then fix the problem, and then there isn't
any problem. I didn't have *a* problem in Washington. I had a
thousand problems, maybe. A million."

"Well, what was the problem that led to your being arrested?"

"I wasn't arrested. Did my parents tell you I was arrested?"

"No," Dr. Adler said. "I'm sorry. They said there was some
trouble with the police."

"So you assumed I was arrested?"

"I suppose I did."

"Well, I wasn't arrested. And the so-called trouble with the
police wasn't my fault. It was my parents'. They got the police involved. They filed a missing persons report. If they hadn't done
that, everything would have been fine. Or finer. Or less bad."

"Were you missing?"

I realized she had tricked me into talking about what had
happened in Washington, and even though I felt okay about
talking about it, I wanted to make it clear I was aware I had been
tricked, so I didn't answer.

After a moment she repeated the question, very quietly, as if
asking it gently would have a better effect.

"Yes," I said. "I was missing."

"For how long?"

"Two days," I said. "It was only two days."

"Two days is a long time to be missing."

"Well, I wasn't missing. I knew where I was."

"Is that what you think 'not missing' means?"

" 'Not missing' means 'found.' "

"And were you found?"

"Eventually. Or not really found. I turned up. I reappeared."

"Where had you been?"

"In Washington. Mostly in the National Gallery. I stayed in a hotel for two nights."

"So you left the seminar?"

"Yes."

"Why?"

"Because I thought if I stayed there I would kill myself."

"Why? What was so bad about the seminar that made you feel that way?"

"I told you. It wasn't just one thing. Or two things. Or twenty things. It was a million things. It was everything. Every moment hurt. I hated every moment."

Dr. Adler was quiet. She was holding her hands in that way she liked to hold her hands, her fingers extended, each fingertip touching its correspondent, waiting patiently for me to continue.

9

April 2003

WEDNESDAY NIGHT WAS "ENTERTAINMENT NIGHT: OUT ON
the Town!" As opposed to Monday, which was CIA night, or
Tuesday, which was "On the Ground, in the Air, Undersea:
Armed Forces Night." I actually don't know how I survived until
Wednesday, for The American Classroom was unbearable from
the very first moments.

In the hotel room I unfolded the cot that was by process of
elimination to be mine, and I felt immediately infantilized and
put at a disadvantage. My roommates, Dakin (Dakin sat beside
me at dinner that night, and in what I thought was an inspired
attempt to engage him in conversation, I asked him if he knew
that Tennessee Williams's younger brother was named Dakin. I
knew that because I read Williams's memoir [which is called
Memoirs] and I remembered I thought Dakin would be a good
name for a dog [at least better than Miró]. Anyway, when I men-

tioned this to Dakin he looked at me kind of blankly and asked me if Tennessee Williams was a country singer. [I think he was thinking of Tennessee Ernie Ford.] I told him no, Tennessee Williams was a playwright, and Dakin looked at me like I was crazy and trying to trick him in some way, and turned away and never spoke to me again) and Thomas, sat on their adult-sized beds and watched me. I opened my cot and sort of tossed my suitcase on it in what I thought was an impressively casual masculine way, but the weight of the suitcase caused the two ends to snap back together with an alarming vehemence, swallowing my suitcase and startling me. "Goodness," I said.

I don't know why I said Goodness. I never say Goodness. My grandmother says Goodness, but I don't think I have ever said it in my life (as an exclamation, I mean), but there was something about the whole situation that had completely unnerved me and so I said Goodness. As soon as I said it I realized how imbecilic it sounded, and I heard my roommates chuckling behind me in that snorting way that always indicates you are being laughed at, not with. I thought about saying Shit or Fuck or Fucking Shit but I knew saying that would only intensify by contrast the patheticness of Goodness. So I said nothing, and cracked the cot back open emphatically, so it stuck.

It was, as they say, downhill from there. There were a hundred representatives participating in The American Classroom, two from each state, and we were divided into two parties, the Washingtons and the Jeffersons. Two buses took us everywhere—the Washingtons rode in one while the Jeffersons rode in the other—and there was a lot of inane cheering and pounding on the windows when one bus overtook the other. I don't understand this propensity to turn everything, like driving from the Russell Senate Office Building to Taco Bell, into a competition.

We were encouraged to sit beside a different person every time we rode the bus, but on our very first trip (to the Capitol on Monday morning) a cadre of students who thought they were, and therefore were perceived as being, cool sat in the back of the bus and clearly claimed the territory. As an urban student who had taken the subway to school ever since I entered fifth grade, the whole world of school buses was foreign to me. I found it rather fascinating, in an anthropological kind of way. Whenever we got back on the bus there was this covert rush to get a seat near the back of the bus, which was interesting to watch because of course it was uncool to appear as though you wanted to be cool enough to sit in the back and uncool to look as if you needed to rush to get a back seat, because if you were genuinely cool the ineluctable rules of the universe would ensure you sat in the back. I usually sat very near the front of the bus with a girl named Sue Kenney from Pennsylvania. She was an earnest, hefty gal who could have used more (or some) deodorant, but she loved everything and everyone and was having THE BEST TIME OF HER LIFE! She seemed in many ways to be the polar opposite of me and in an odd way this seemed to ideally suit us to each other. She didn't seem to notice that I barely said ten words to her, for she was constantly prattling and pointing out interesting things outside the window that we had just passed. I actually grew fond of her in a nastily superior kind of way, for she was so completely artless and optimistic and clueless, she didn't care that she smelled bad or was fat or wore clothes unlike everyone else's, she had some weird disconnect with life that kept her constantly bubbling, and you knew she would go blithely through her long horribly boring life thinking everything was just swell (the opposite of me).

Nothing was swell for me. Mealtimes were the worst. Breakfast was fine—a buffet in the hotel's Excelsior "Ballroom" at which many people chose not to appear, so there were many empty tables, and even if you had to sit at a table with someone, they didn't expect you to say anything besides good morning, and that I could handle. I wish the whole day were like breakfast, when people are still connected to their dreams, focused inward, and not yet ready to engage with the world around them. I realized this is how I am all day; for me, unlike other people, there doesn't come a moment after a cup of coffee or a shower or whatever when I suddenly feel alive and awake and connected to the world. If it were always breakfast, I would be fine. In what I assumed to be an effort to keep us fatigued and subsequently more manageable, we were not allowed to sleep until late at night and were awakened early in the morning. We didn't return to the hotel until about 11:00, and then there was an ice-cream social (once again in the "Ballroom") where people could sing or play their guitars or read their poetry or juggle tennis balls or egotistically display other so-called talents. Then there was a lot of running up and down the hallways and shrieking and boys running into girls' rooms and vice versa, all of which inevitably resulted in the regurgitation of ice cream. "Lights Out" was at 12:30. Breakfast was from 7:00 to 8:00, and the buses left the parking lot every morning at 8:30 sharp.

Lunch and dinner were awful. We ate at places like Olive Garden or Red Lobster, usually in our own special rooms with special menus to choose from. I learned very quickly it was much easier for me to be the first to sit at a table and let others join me, because there was something about sitting down at a table that was already populated, especially if it meant sitting down beside someone, that I couldn't do. I know when you sit beside someone for lunch in a Red Lobster, it's not like you're marrying them or imposing yourself on them forever, but if I did sit down beside someone I felt this awful obligation to be charming or at least have something to say, and the pressure of having to be charming (or merely verbal) incapacitates me. But there was something about being the one sat next to that diffused some of the tension, for in that case I did not feel I was imposing myself upon someone but rather accommodating someone else's presence (or imposition). But really it was all generally horrible and got worse every meal, and this was combined with a thousand other moments of feeling fundamentally and entirely alienated, so that by Wednesday night—*Entertainment Night!*—I had sort of lost my grip on whatever sense of normalcy I had arrived with. I remember at one point (genuinely) wondering if I was, perhaps, genetically altered in some way, some tiny modification of DNA that separated me from the species in some slight but essential way, the way mules can mate with donkeys but not with horses (I think). It seemed that everyone else could mate, could fit their parts together in pleasant and productive ways, but that some almost indistinguishable difference in my anatomy and psyche set me slightly, yet irrevocably, apart.

It was a troubling thing to feel, and it made me sad. It made me cry in the men's room of the Russell Senate Office Building. It made me not want to be alive.

On Entertainment Night! we had a choice of going to a comedy club or a dinner theater. I decided on the dinner theater because I had never been to one and I hate stand-up comics; I think funny is something you are, not something you desperately try to be in front of a roomful of obnoxious people.

As we drove back to the hotel late Wednesday afternoon to prepare for our evenings on the town, Sue Kenney said to me, "I'm so excited!"

I was looking out the window at the garbage that was strewn along the breakdown lane. Most of it made sense—soda cans, the detritus of fast-food meals, newspapers—but every once in a while there'd be something alarming, like a child's red boot, a birdcage, a suitcase burst open, disgorging its contents. And it bothered me because each of these objects was on the shoulder of the highway for a reason, something or some things had happened to cause someone to toss a child's boot out the window, and I felt like we were rushing past story after story, and that each story was sad. And I was thinking about this, and trying to think positively, trying to imagine a happy scenario for the odd objects I passed—a little girl had just been bought beautiful new boots, and the old ones were gleefully discarded; someone had packed for a trip to the hospital but on their way had been called by the doctor to say that it was all a mistake, their liver was not riddled with cancer, they should go home, and, undone by joy, had thrown their suitcase out the window. I was trying to put a happy face on the discarded birdcage when Sue Kenney spoke, so for a moment I didn't answer, and she said, "Don't you want to know why I'm excited?" She said this very pleasantly, as if it was perfectly normal to prompt someone this way, and I suppose for her it was.

I said, "Yes—tell me."

"I'm wearing my evening pajamas tonight! I'm so excited!"

"What are evening pajamas?" I asked.

"Oh, you don't know? I thought you would, coming from New York City and all. They're an alternative to formal gowns. A sort of tunic worn over flowing pants. Mine are electric blue with a beaded bodice. I can't wait to put them on!"

"So you're going to the dinner theater?" Evening pajamas sounded a bit posh for the comedy club.

"Oh no," Sue Kenney said. "I'm going to the symphony. At the Kennedy Center."

"I thought we had to choose between the comedy club and the dinner theater?"

"Yes, but if those aren't suitable for you, you can go to the symphony."

"What do you mean—not suitable?"

"Well, they usually make dirty jokes about sex in comedy clubs. And use filthy language. And when my parents found out the play we were going to see promoted deviant lifestyles, they complained to the mucky-mucks and now I get to go to the sym-

phony. Apparently there are eight of us going. I don't have anything against popular culture and all that dirty stuff, I'd just
much rather not drag my mind through the sewer."

When we got back to the hotel I asked one of the "mucky-
mucks" if I could switch and go to the symphony and she said
no, the symphony tickets were only for those people who had
moral or religious objections to comedy or theater, and since I
had signed up for the theater I obviously was fine with it, and besides, there were no more tickets.

Both Dakin and Thomas had opted for the comedy club, and
I could tell they thought it was faggy to go to the dinner theater.
I wished I could figure out a way not to go to either, to just stay
alone in my hotel room for the evening reading (Trollope's *Can
You Forgive Her?*), but they were very paranoid about losing someone, and the buses would never leave until it was confirmed that
everyone was on board. So I went out and boarded the theater-
bound bus. I got on early so I could be sat next to rather than
sit next to, but it turned out that more people had opted for
the comedy club (surprise) so I had a seat to myself. I saw Sue
Kenney huffing past in her evening pajamas, which looked like a
cross between pajamas and a warm-up suit. I watched her disappear into a van with the other folk who chose not to drag their
minds through the sewers of contemporary comedy and drama.

There was something undeniably high-spirited about the
scene in the parking lot. This was the one night when the American Classroom dress code was not in effect, and you could tell
that everyone was feeling liberated. All the girls, like Sue Kenney,

were wearing outfits specially bought for the evening, outfits that they thought revealed them in the best possible way, and so they felt perfectly revealed, and this knowledge imbued them with a confidence and gaiety that was almost palpable. And the boys were all clean, their faces freshly and brutally shaved, their hair painstakingly gelled into exquisite apparent carelessness, with this electric feeling inside them, which matched the feelings in the girls, that they were all ascending, moving into a future that could only improve them, and I wondered what it was like—the miracle, the stupidity of feeling that.

I thought dinner theater meant that you paid one price for dinner and theater, but I didn't realize you did them simultaneously. I actually thought we would have dinner in one room and then go into the theater, so I was surprised to see that the tables were in the theater. I thought that only happened in Las Vegas, where I assumed it was okay to eat while watching tigers and showgirls perform, but I couldn't imagine eating in front of actors. It seemed to me about the rudest thing you could do. Even if they turned the houselights down, there'd be the noise of the entire audience chewing.

The tables were arranged on terraced platforms and we were instructed to sit at any table on the top two. The platforms below us were filled with mostly middle-aged women who stared unhappily at us as we passed through their midst. Most of the tables were for four or six or eight but there were a few tables on the uppermost platform for two and I knew if I sat at one of them no one would sit with me, and I was right: no one did.

In lieu of proper menus, small cards at each place setting proclaimed:

Welcome American Classroom!
Tonights [*sic*] Menu

Overture
Minestrone Soup or Filed [*sic*] Green Salads

Act 1
Chicken Paprika, Vegetable Compost [*sic*], Rice Pilaf

INTERMISSION

Coffee or Tea

Act 2
Chocolate Zum-Zums drizzled with Raspberry Coulis

Note:
*Vegetarians are welcome to exchange their Chicken for an
additional serving of rice or vegetables
Please notify your server*

A frail and elderly waitress approached me with a pitcher of water in one hand and a pitcher of what looked like iced tea in the other. They were apparently heavy, for she strained to keep them both aloft. I had a vision of both her hands snapping off at the wrists.

"Iced tea or water." She attempted to raise each pitcher as she named its contents, but the gesture was extremely subtle.

"Water, please," I said.

As she poured the water in my glass she said, "And would you like soup or salad. You can't have both."

"May I ask you a question?"

She put both pitchers down on the table and wrung her hands. "What?" she said, unencouragingly.

"What are filed greens?"

"What?"

"It says here there's a salad of filed greens. Can you tell me what they are?" I pointed to the word on the card, but she didn't look at it.

"I don't know," she said. "It's your basic salad. Lettuce. I'd recommend the soup."

"I'll have the filed greens," I said. I had wanted to ask her about the vegetable compost and the Zum-Zums, but before I could she said, "Suit yourself," hoisted her pitchers, and moved to the next table.

The first course was served quickly and almost immediately cleared, replaced with plates of chicken paprika, vegetable compost, and rice pilaf. The compost was simply that familiar and depressing medley of frozen carrots, corn, and lima beans. What made the rice a pilaf remained a mystery. As soon as everyone was served their entrées, the waitresses scurried away and the lights went down, and it was so dark you couldn't even see your plate, let alone eat off it. Then a recorded voice welcomed us to the theater and reminded everyone to turn off their cell phones (which I found pretty ironic, given that we would be eating dinner throughout the performance). And then the curtain rose and the houselights were bumped up a bit so you could see to eat, and the play began.

The deviant play we were seeing was the female version of *The Odd Couple*, starring two middle-aged actresses who had once had respectable careers in movies, followed by less-respected careers playing moms on sitcoms, and then had disappeared for a while. I wondered if this was just another step on their descent into obscurity or if perhaps they had hit bottom and starring in a dinner theater production of *The Odd Couple* was the beginning of a comeback. And I wondered if it was their need of money or their desire for fame that prompted them to perform in this production. There was something very dignified and brave and sad about the entire thing—the idea of what people can be reduced to, how variable one's life is, and the awful things people do to survive—a poignant subtext that was at complete odds with the play itself. This made watching it an upsetting experience.

And since I was on the top platform, by watching the play I also watched the audience. During the first ten or fifteen minutes everyone maintained an almost devotional raptness, but as the act continued, attention drifted away from the stage. People started eating their food, whispering to their neighbor, or not whispering to the person across the table from them. Every so often someone would hiss a piercing *shush* and silence would fall, but like a fire that had been insufficiently doused, the sounds of talking and eating would slowly flicker back into being.

When the act ended, everyone clapped madly to make up for

their inattention, and then the ladies all got up and stampeded toward the women's room. I needed to use the restroom, too, but before I could get up a strange thing happened. This girl named Nareem Jabbar, who was the other delegate from New York State, came up and sat down at my table. I actually sort of liked Nareem. She lived in Schenectady and was very smart and often asked unsettling questions at the conclusion of seminars.

She sat down in the chair across from me and said, "James, what are you doing?"

I wasn't aware she knew my name, and she spoke to me as if we were very old, tight friends. I was disoriented. So I said nothing.

"James, James," she said. "Talk to me. What are you doing, sitting here all alone?"

"What do you mean?" I asked. One of the reasons why I hate to talk to people is that when I am forced to talk I inevitably say something stupid.

"You're always alone," she said. "You're sitting here all by yourself. We can't have that. Come join us."

This is something I really hate. Really, really hate—when people react to your being alone as some kind of problem for them. I knew the only reason she wanted me to come and sit at her table was that she wanted to do someone a favor. My sitting alone bothered her; it's like how you resent those people standing up on the subway when you're seated. It's like they're standing up just to make you feel bad. Sometimes there are even some seats available—half seats between big men with spread legs—but they won't sit in them, they just stand in front of you and look exhausted and miserable and make you feel terrible because you're sitting down. And I knew Nareem just wanted me to sit at her table because I was like some eyesore that prevented her from enjoying the show. I find it disturbing that so much seemingly altruistic behavior is really quite selfish. Even so-called saints like Mother Teresa bother me. In some ways she was just as ambitious as people like my father or anyone who wants to be at the top of their profession. Mother Teresa wanted to be the best saint, the top saint, so she did the most disgusting things she could do, and I know she helped people and relieved suffering and I'm not saying that's bad, I'm just saying I think she was as selfish and ambitious as everyone else. The problem with thinking this way is that if you want to avoid this kind of ambition and selfishness you should do absolutely nothing—do no harm, but do no good either. Do nothing: don't presume to interfere with the world. I know this makes practically no sense, but it's what I was thinking when Nareem sat down at my table.

She must have sensed in my silence some sort of judgment or wariness (or idiocy), for she looked at me with genuine puzzlement, as if I might be a deaf-mute or something, and said, very slowly and distinctly, "There is room at our table. Would you like to join us?"

And then I realized she was really being nice. She was sincerely being nice. She was misguided, but she was being nice. But she didn't know what she was saying, she was saying come sit at our table as if that was something I could do. As if I could get up and sit down at her table and become a person sitting at her table. As if becoming a person sitting at her table only involved getting up and walking down a platform and sitting at her table.

"No, thank you," I said. "I'm fine alone."

"So you're a loser?" she said.

"What?" I couldn't believe she had called me a loser.

"You're a loner," she said. "You like to be alone."

"Yes," I said.

"Well, that's cool," she said. "As long as you're happy. But please feel free to join us whenever you'd like. Isn't this play just about the suckiest thing you've ever seen?"

"Yes," I said.

She sat there looking at me for a moment, and I could tell she was trying to decide if she should try to prolong our conversation—"draw me out," I suppose—but apparently she decided I was beyond help. She stood up and returned to her table of laughing happy normal boys and girls.

I realized I had to get out of there. I stood up and passed through the tables. The lobby was full of happy chattering ladies. Outside the door a few people stood about smoking, hungrily sucking the nicotine out of their cigarettes. One of them was the congressman's wife who had met my group at the train station. It had only been three days ago, but it seemed like ages. It's weird how slowly time passes when you're miserable.

"Where are you going?" she called to me as I passed by.

"Just for a little stroll," I said. "To get some fresh air."

"Well, don't go too far," she said. "We don't want to lose you."

I ran out into the middle of the parking lot and stood there for a moment, hidden between two hulking SUVs. I felt as if I had escaped from a house on fire; I was actually panting, and I thought if I turned around I would feel the hot bright conflagration of the strip mall. So I did not turn around, I ran across the parking lot and into the field behind it. I walked toward the center of the field—it wasn't really a field, it might have been a field once, but now it was just a sort of open, abandoned, useless garbagy space. I thought how the center is defined by the spot farthest from every point of the perimeter. Since it wasn't a very big field it did not take me long to reach its (supposed) center. I unzipped and peed fiercely, proudly, into the ground, as if that was the one thing I could do well. Then I looked around. The four sides of the field were bounded by the strip mall's parking lot; a highway; a row of identical subdivision houses, the back of each exactly the same, except each house had a different pattern of lighted windows, like patterns of Braille spelling out different messages: baby's asleep, daddy's home, nobody's home; and a long line of trees, obscuring whatever lay beyond them. I felt I was presented with four choices, four different places to go, and as I did not want to return to the theater, or look into the lighted windows of the subdivision, or expose myself to the glare and gore of the highway, the only remaining choice was the trees, and I ran toward them, before anyone could come chasing after me and force me back into the theater.

The trees were more substantial than I expected, and actually amassed themselves into something resembling a forest. Unlike the field, which was littered with the revolting effluvia of human lives, the forest seemed, at least in the dark, to be pristine. I don't know why, but I often think about when any particular patch of ground was last touched by human feet or hands or regarded by human eyes. In the city, there's a small area on the corner of LaGuardia Place and Houston Street that has been fenced in and allowed to return to its primordial state, before the Dutch bought Manhattan from the Indians for $24. I like to look at it when I pass by, although it just looks like an overgrown abandoned lot. But I always have this feeling that I'll see something startling inside the fence—a fox or a turtle or a coyote or some animal that has miraculously returned to this little pristine patch of land. I think it's because I want to know that time can move backward as well as forward. That we could return to that moment when Manhattan was, in F. Scott Fitzgerald's words, "a fresh, green breast of the new world," not the dirty brown crotch it is now. So I look every time I pass by, but usually all I see is Snapple bottles, used condoms, and losing Lotto tickets.

I walked deeper into the woods, down a slope, and into a sort of culvert, through which trickled a narrow stream. The stream smelled a little funky and I was glad it was dark, so I couldn't see how polluted it was. I felt very weird and shaky and I couldn't stop thinking of the strip mall in flames, so I squatted down and covered my face, pushing the heels of my hands into the sockets of my eyes. They fit perfectly, like two halves of a whole, and my hands were exactly the right size to cradle my skull. It seemed like another example of how well human beings are designed, that you were shaped to comfort yourself. I held myself like that and made a humming crooning sound that further removed me from the world.

After a while I remembered about the dinner theater and

the bus and The American Classroom and the rest of my life. I had planned to return to the parking lot and wait until the play was over and get back on the bus with everyone else, but I knew in some weird way that by running away from the theater I had run away from much more than that, and that it was an irreversible action, that I had severed myself from The American Classroom as surely as if I had, like a fox caught in a trap, gnawed off a limb to limp away.

I knew that once in the bus they would realize I was missing, and Susan Porter Wright would remember seeing me at intermission, and I didn't know what they would do, but I thought it best to get as far away from there as I could.

So I jumped over the little stream and climbed up the opposite side of the culvert and bushwhacked through the dark forest. I climbed over a chain-link fence into someone's backyard. In the darkness I could make out a swing set a few feet in front of me, with a slide and two regular swings and one little kiddy one. And then I saw a baby sitting in that swing, toppled to one side, and I thought, Oh my God, someone's left a baby in the swing! Then as I got closer I realized it wasn't a baby, it was a doll. I felt like a moron and looked around as if someone might have been watching me and intuiting my thoughts. But there was no one around. I sat the doll up straight and gave the swing a hard push. At the apex of its flight the doll leaped out and flew brilliantly through the air and crash-landed on her skull in the middle of the lawn.

I left it there and moved closer to the house, toward the one large window that was lighted on the first floor. I crept near enough to see inside, into a family room or den or rec room or something wholesome like that. A man and a woman were sitting on the floor playing a board game and behind them a golden retriever was sleeping on a sofa. The TV was on, but I could just see the light from the screen, I couldn't tell what they were watching. Whatever it was, they didn't seem to be paying attention: they were very involved in their game, clapping their hands and laughing. They looked like they were in a commercial for that game, demonstrating how much fun it was. I could only see the man from the back, but the woman was facing me. She was about forty and was wearing a bathrobe and had her hair pulled back from her face with a hair band. She really seemed to be enjoying the game, and I thought it was odd and a little creepy that a husband and wife would be playing a board game at ten o'clock on a Wednesday night. I didn't have much experience of life in the suburbs, but I didn't think it was as wholesome as all that. Then it occurred to me that it might be one of those erotic board games couples play to restore passion to their sexless marriages. I once had the horrifying experience of finding such a game ("Keep the US in Lust") beneath my parents' bed. But the game this couple was playing didn't look very sexy: they were throwing dice and moving little men around the board, counting squares. Then the dog raised his head and looked directly at me through the window and softly woofed. "Oh, hush, Horace," the woman said to the dog. She was counting out spaces on the board and didn't look up, but the man turned around and looked at me, and I saw that it wasn't a man. It was a teenage boy with Down syndrome. He stared at me for a moment with his odd disturbing eyes, looking right at me, but I don't think he could see me standing outside in the darkness. Then the dog barked again and the boy said something to his mother, and she stood up and moved toward the window and I stepped farther back into the darkness. She leaned toward the window and cupped her hands against the dark glass and peered out. I backed farther away and then ran around the side of the house and down the driveway into the street.

I ran quite a ways up the street because I wanted to get away from that house. Everything about it spooked me—the doll left out in the swing, the husband turning into a retarded son, and the scared way the mother peered out the window. The neighborhood was deserted but brightly lit with humming streetlights that seemed more like searchlights. As I turned the corner I saw a man walking a dog on the sidewalk in front of me, so I crossed the street and kept running, but the man must have been one of those neighborhood patrol alarmists because he shouted something and began chasing me. The dog barked. At the corner I saw a bus pull up to a bus shelter and open its door. A fat woman carrying a lot of shopping bags toddled down the steps and I thought, If I keep running and get on the bus the man with the dog will think I am just running for the bus and not running away from the scene of a crime, which in a way I felt I was doing because of what had happened at the spooky house. I knew I wouldn't get arrested for trespassing and watching people play a board game through a window, but nonetheless I felt guilty, as if I had done something criminal.

10

June 2003

I DIDN'T SAY ANYTHING FOR A MOMENT; I JUST STARED AT DR. Adler's bookshelves. I noticed she had relocated *The Age of Innocence* from its hiding place on the bottom shelf to one of the upper shelves. I wondered if there was some message for me in this gesture or if it was just a random act. Probably whoever cleaned her office put it there.

"And then what happened?" Dr. Adler asked.

"What do you mean?"

"I think you know perfectly well what I mean. It's a fairly straightforward question."

"I know. I didn't really mean what, I meant why: Why would you ask me that question? If I wanted to tell you what happened next, I would."

"Would you? I'm not sure you would."

"Why wouldn't I?"

Dr. Adler sighed wearily, which I thought was an unprofessional thing for a psychiatrist to do. "I think you're smart enough to know what you're doing," she said. "And I don't think it's helping you, or us. In fact, that's probably why you're doing it."

I looked at her. She had never made pronouncements like this before, and I was startled. She looked directly back at me, her expression hard and clear and unvarying.

"You make it very difficult for people to talk to you, sometimes. Often, in fact. You create obstacles. Why do you think you do that?"

"Because I don't want people to talk to me," I said.

"Why?"

"I don't know. I just don't."

"I think you do," she said.

"Can we just forget this? Can I just tell you what happened next?"

"You can forget anything you want. You can tell me anything you want."

"What if I want to forget everything and tell you nothing?"

"Then I suppose that, among other things, you should stop coming here to see me." She leaned back in her chair—I hadn't noticed that at some point she had leaned forward. She crossed her arms and looked at me gently, patiently, as if we could sit like that forever. She smiled slightly, as if she remembered something fairly pleasant from a long time ago.

I don't know why, but it was a nice moment. One of those moments when everything seems to be in its place. The pencils in the Guggenheim Museum coffee mug on her desk, how they fell away from each other at varying angles and directions, like those apparently casual beautiful flower arrangements that are actually the result of much artful expertise—I had a notion of them being the center of the universe and everything spreading out around them, all the other items on the desk, the office, the building, the block, the city, and the world beyond.

"I feel very good about where everything is," I said.

She nodded as if she understood what I was talking about.

"What happened next was that the bus drove back into D.C. and I got out in a nice neighborhood with lots of nice hotels and I went into the nicest and used my mother's credit card to check in. I was worried because I had no suitcase and in movies hotel clerks are always suspicious of people checking in with no bags, but it didn't seem to be a problem at this hotel. And then I took the elevator upstairs and used my little key card to get in the room, and it was just like a hotel room should be, it was very clean and still and quiet and there was something about the stillness and the quiet that made me feel weird, like I shouldn't speak or move or I would disturb the room. I wanted to be as quiet and still as the room. I wanted to be as little in the room as possible. To have the least effect on the room I could have. So I lay down very carefully on the bed, trying not to muss the comforter.

"I lay on the bed and thought about what I had done. I knew that leaving the theater was bad, not getting back on the bus was bad, but there was nothing I could do about it now. So I did nothing. I thought the best thing to do would be nothing, and in that way things couldn't get any worse. I kept thinking about that oath that doctors take: First, do no harm, and I kept saying it to myself, over and over, *first do no harm, first do no harm, first do no harm,* and that was fine because I didn't want to do anything or think anything, and at some point I fell asleep.

"I spent most of the next day wandering around D.C. I was a little afraid I might run into The American Classroom somewhere, or they would drive by and someone in one of the buses would look out the window and see me, but then I realized that would never happen. That I was alone and no one could find me. No one knew where I was or who I was. It was a beautiful day, I remember, warm and springlike, everything green and blooming. The trees had new leaves, clean, fresh new leaves, like baby lettuce. Filed greens.

"When it got dark I went back to the hotel, and had dinner in the restaurant. It was a very bad fancy restaurant, but luckily I had my American Classroom clothes on, so I looked like a nice young man and I remember sitting alone and having this very expensive (bad) dinner and thinking that other people in the restaurant were looking at me and wondering who I was, what I was doing there, eating alone.

"And then I went up to the room and slept the same as the night before, on top of the comforter. I think I thought that if I didn't leave any evidence of being in the hotel room I could somehow claim I had never been there. That my mother couldn't get angry at me for using her credit card to charge a three-hundred-dollar hotel room if I had only barely experienced it, hadn't used the towels or the whirlpool bathtub or the complimentary organic bath products scented with ylang-ylang, hadn't lain between the four-hundred-thread-count sheets or watched soft-core porn on my in-room entertainment center." I paused. "Is my time almost up?"

Dr. Adler looked past me, as if she could tell time by gazing into the future, but I knew she was only looking at the clock that was strategically placed on the bookshelf facing her. "No," she said. "Why?"

"Because I don't want to start talking about what happened the next day if there isn't time."

"Don't worry about that. There isn't a patient after you. What happened the next day?"

"The next day I got up and had breakfast at Au Bon Pain and read *The Washington Post*. There was a small article about me being missing and a photo. The caption under the photo was 'James Sveck: Missing Misfit.'"

"Are you making that up?" Dr. Adler asked.

"No," I said. "It's the truth. I was the missing misfit. Google it if you don't believe me. They interviewed Nareem Jabbar because she was the last person to speak with me, and she said I was a misfit. Actually she said I didn't fit in, but 'James Sveck: He Didn't Fit In and He's Missing' isn't a good caption."

"Okay," she said. "Go on."

I paused for a moment because I didn't like the way she was directing me. "I knew no one would recognize me because the picture in the paper was my yearbook photo from junior year, when I was experimenting with long hair. I have to admit I did look rather like a misfit.

"After breakfast I went to the National Gallery. I love how the National Gallery is free. You can walk in and walk out and walk back in. When I find something good like that (which is practically never), I try to take advantage of it, so I'd go out one door and back in at another entrance because it felt so good to enter a museum for free. Anyway I spent a lot of time in the museum. It was odd, like I had never been in a museum before. It just seemed weird that you could walk in and look at all these old, beautiful, valuable paintings. You could look at them closely, with nothing between you and the painting. And I was going very slowly, looking at every painting, and I felt that there was something beautiful about each one. Even the ugly still lifes of dead fish or lynched rabbits, or the bloody religious paintings, if you just looked at little pieces of them, like a single square inch, the paint was beautiful, and I kept thinking about the difference between these rooms of paintings and the dinner theater and how good the paintings made me feel about life and how bad the dinner theater made me feel. And I knew life was not about a choice between the National Gallery and a dinner theater, but I felt that it was in some way, that the two couldn't coexist, that if you had a world with these paintings in it, hung in these beautiful rooms that anyone could walk in off the street and see, then how could there also be TV moms acting in a terrible play while people watched them and ate chicken paprika? I suppose most people would think that it was wonderful, that the world is so varied, that there is something for everyone, and I don't know why I felt so closed and bitter and threatened by things I did not like. I knew I was fucked up and I thought: *misfit, misfit*.

"Then I walked into a small room with only four paintings, and I remembered those paintings from the last time I had been in the National Gallery, which was on my eighth-grade class trip to Washington. They are by Thomas Cole and are called *The Voyage of Life*. Have you seen them?"

"No," she said. "I don't believe I have."

"This is embarrassing because they're very sentimental, hokey, kind of stupid paintings. They depict the four ages of man: childhood, youth, manhood, and old age. In each one a figure in a boat is floating down a river and is guided by an angel. In the first one, there's a little baby in the boat, and the boat is emerging from a dark cave. The womb. It's early morning and the stream flows calmly through an idyllic valley full of flowers. The angel is in the boat, standing up behind the baby, and they both have their arms stretched out to embrace the world before them. In the *Youth* painting it's noon and the boat has moved farther into the beautiful valley. The baby has morphed into a young lad and he's standing up, reaching out toward the future. The angel is hovering on the bank, pointing the way like a traffic guard. The clouds have formed themselves into a fantastic castle in the air, surrounded by blue sky. In the *Manhood* painting the stream has turned into a raging river, and the landscape is rocky and barren. It's dusk and the sky is full of storm clouds. The youth is now a man and he's still standing up in the boat, but now his hands are clasped in prayer as the boat heads toward the rapids. The angel is far away, looking down through a hole in the clouds, watching the boat as it plunges forward. It's very creepy. In the final painting the boat enters from the opposite side of the canvas. It's hard to say what time it is, because the sky is full of dark clouds except for far in the distance, where there are shafts of light falling.

It's some twilit time outside of time. The river is about to flow calmly into a huge dark sea. An old man sits in the boat and the angel floats right above him, pointing toward the dark sea and sky. In the distance another angel looks down from the clouds. The old man's hands are still clasped, but it is hard to know if he's praying, or beseeching the angel to save him before he floats off into the huge creepy darkness."

I paused.

"You know those paintings very well," said Dr. Adler.

"When I first saw them, when I was in eighth grade, I thought they were wonderful. They seemed very profound. I bought prints of them, one of each, in the gift shop. Not postcards, but actual prints. I used the money my mother had given me to buy souvenirs, and I brought them home and put them in cheap frames and hung them over my desk. *Childhood* and *Youth* on top and *Manhood* and *Old Age* beneath. And I liked to look at them. They're very formulaic, but I liked that, I liked to see how the elements changed from one to another. How the clouds were castles in one and thunderheads in the next. How the fertile valley became a rocky wasteland. And then one day this kid named Andrew Mooney came over after school and he saw the paintings and told me they were stupid and faggy, so I took them down. I think I threw them away. Anyway, I forgot about them."
I paused.

"Yes . . ." Dr. Adler murmured.

"I was shocked when I saw them again, exactly as they had been, in the same little room. I couldn't believe that such hokey paintings would be on permanent view at the National Gallery.

And then I had the irrational feeling that they had not been, that
somehow someone knew I was coming back and had just rehung
them. That it was some sort of trap or something. But I knew
that wasn't true. I knew that they had hung there—I guess it was
only five years, but it seemed like a very long time. You can't go
backward in time, I know that. But that's what I felt I had done.
Everything else sort of dropped away, those five years and the entire world, and I felt like I was two people. Seriously. I could feel
what I felt when I was thirteen looking at the paintings, and I
could feel what I felt then. I stayed in the room for a very long
time. I kept thinking, I should go now, but I didn't. A guard kept
coming in and looking at me. And then I got upset because I realized I wanted to be in the last painting, *Old Age*. I wanted to be
in the boat floating into darkness. I wanted to skip the *Manhood*
boat. The man in that boat looked terrified, and I couldn't understand what the point was: why crash through those treacher-
ous rapids along a river that only flowed into darkness, death? I
wanted to be in the boat with the old man, with all the danger
behind, with the angel near me, guiding me toward death. I
wanted to die.

"I don't really remember, but I think I started to cry, because
the guard came over and made me sit down and people gathered
around me as if I were a painting and looked at me and then another guard came over and tried to take me away and I got belligerent and I tried to run away and I kicked a hole in the wall
and the guard chased me and a man in the next gallery tackled
me. I think he thought I had stolen or defaced a painting. And
the guard took me away, downstairs into an awful little office

with no windows, only a fat woman guard eating her disgusting Taco Bell lunch. And somehow they figured out I was the Missing Misfit. And then the cops came and took me to the police station and I stayed there until my father came to get me and we took a train back to New York that night.

"On the train my father asked me what had happened. And I told him I wasn't happy, so I had run away, and he said *Blah blah blah you can't always run away from things you don't like. That's not how life works.* And I told him that he didn't know me or understand me, that I wasn't unhappy like that, I was unhappy like I wanted to die. He didn't say anything else after that, he just patted my leg and went to the bar car and bought three of those little bottles of Johnnie Walker."

I paused. Dr. Adler didn't say anything. She looked a little spacey. I waited for her to say something but she just sat there.

"I had to write a letter to The American Classroom apologizing for the trouble I caused and I had to pay $213.78 to the National Gallery to repair the hole in the wall. Nareem Jabbar wrote me a note apologizing for calling me a misfit. She said she meant it in the best possible way, that she meant I didn't fit in because I was an individual, not a misfit."

Dr. Adler didn't say anything. She was wearing a charm bracelet with lots of little trinkets hanging off it and she was slowly twirling it around her wrist like a Ferris wheel. After a moment she saw me watching and stopped. She gave the bracelet a little shake and folded her hands in her lap.

I said, "So is my time up?"

This time she looked at her watch. "Yes," she said. "I suppose it is."

I stood up and went to the door.

"Are you okay?" she asked me.

"Of course," I said. "Why wouldn't I be okay?"

"There are lots of reasons why you might not be okay."

"There are lots of reasons why anyone might not be okay," I said.

"Yes," she said, "but that doesn't mean that you're okay."

I was still standing by the door. She did a strange thing. She stood and walked over to me, and reached around me and opened the door. With her other hand she touched me, very lightly, on the center of my back, and kept her hand there until I passed through the door. To an observer it would have appeared as if she was pushing me out the door, but she wasn't pushing me. I could tell by the lightness of her touch that she was not.

II

Monday, July 28, 2003

SINCE THE GALLERY WAS CLOSED ON SATURDAYS AND SUNDAYS during the summer, my mother insisted on keeping it open on Mondays, because she thought galleries that were only open four days a week weren't "serious." On the Monday after her premature return from her honeymoon, both John and my mother had spent most of the day lurking in their offices behind closed doors. No one had set foot in the gallery, and at about two o'clock the sky went dark in a weird green swampy way that gave me a creepy end-of-the-world feeling. Suddenly it began to pour. The water lashed against the large windows like badly faked movie rain, and I went over and looked down at the people in the street scurrying for shelter. After a moment the street was empty. When I sat back down I saw that a little window had opened on my computer screen, with a message in it: *Hello.*

I returned the salutation. A moment later the following message appeared: *Just wanted to say I like your profile.*

I wrote, *What profile?*

On Gent4Gent: Hot and Bothered. I'm Black Narcissus. Check out my profile?

Okay. I realized it was John. He had apparently found the profile I had created last week. For a moment I considered typing, *John, it's me, James :)* , but before I could John had written, *Do you really work at Sotheby's?*

Yes.

Wow, that's cool. I direct a gallery. Chelsea.

Which one?

I can't say. Have to be discreet. :)

That's cool. I understand.

Did you check my profile?

Yes. Very nice.

Thanks. Like yours too. Do you have a pic?

No. Sorry.

It's okay. Your stats are nice.

Thanks. Yours too.

You at work?

Yes.

Me too.

Busy?

No. Very slow. You?

Same here. It's pretty dead this time of year.

Tell me about it.

There was a pause and then I heard John get up and close his door.

Sorry. Just closed the door.

So we're alone now?

LOL. In a manner of speaking. I'm surprised I don't know you. The art world is so small.

Maybe you do.

I don't think so. The only person I know in Contemporary Art at Sotheby's is Kendra Katrovicht.

Well, I'm not Kendra Katrovicht.

Good. Do you know who I am?

What do you mean?

Thought you might know me, or of me. There are so few black guys in the art world.

I don't know any. Is it raining downtown?

Yes. Hard.

Same here.

You're not so far away.

I know. Listen I should get back to work.

Okay. Me too.

Nice chatting with you.

You too. Hope we can stay in touch.

Sure. I'll add you to my favorites.

Same here. Great.

Later, then.

Great. Bye for now.

Bye.

After a few minutes John emerged from his office. I could

feel him standing behind me. And smell him, too: he always smelled nice—a warm, clean scent that made me aware of his skin. "Are you busy?" he asked me.

"Yes," I said. "Very. If you take a number and have a seat I'll be with you shortly."

"Very funny, James. I actually have something for you to do. I'd like you to call Sotheby's and get the names of all the people who work in the Contemporary Art Department. But don't tell them where you're calling from. Don't mention the gallery. Okay?"

"You want me to lie?"

"No," said John. "Just don't tell them."

"What if they ask?"

"Then make something up."

"You mean lie?"

"Yes," said John.

I called Sotheby's and told them I was a fact checker from *The New Yorker* updating our resource database and got the names of all the people who worked in the Contemporary Art Department. I added a few fake names to the list and e-mailed it to John. A few minutes later a message window appeared on my screen.

Hey, it read.

I typed *Hey* back.

Don't mean to stalk you or anything, but I'm going to a party at the Frick this evening and wondered if you maybe wanted to join me?

It hadn't occurred to me that John would actually be interested in meeting—it seemed too weird, that somebody would actually want to meet a person who could, for all intents and purposes, not even be a person.

Sorry, wrote John, *I just thought it might be a good opportunity to meet. But you're probably busy.*

No, I wrote.

I'd just love to meet you. You sound very interesting. I mean apart from all the Gent4Gent nonsense. It's so hard to meet smart, interesting guys.

What makes you think I'm smart and interesting?

Well, I don't know too many stupid, boring men who work at Sotheby's and have studied at the Sorbonne.

I almost wrote: But I don't work at Sotheby's and I haven't studied at the Sorbonne, but then I remembered that I had. And then I thought that if smart, interesting people studied at the Sorbonne and worked at Sotheby's and I had done neither of those things, did that mean I was boring and stupid? I often think in this ridiculously reductive way, which I blame on higher mathematics (not that I got very high), where I was always so eager to pounce upon any solution that arose from the murk of an equation.

You still there? John typed.

Yes.

Good. Thought I scared you away. We can meet some other time if you'd like. Or never. Whatever.

No, I typed. *Tonight is good. I'd like to meet tonight.*

Great. It's a reception for some new Fragonard book. I'll call now and get your name on the list, and then I'll meet you there at 6:30. Is that okay?

Sure. That would be fine. See you then.

Wait, John wrote. *I need to know your name. For the list.*

Oh, right. Philip Braque. This was one of the invented names I had added to the list.

Cool. I'm John Webster. I'll see you there at 6:30. Let's meet in the courtyard. Near the fountain. I'll be easy to spot.

How?

I'll be the only black man there.

You never know, I wrote.

Believe me, I know. So see you at 6:30.

Great. See you there.

Really looking forward to meeting you. See you soon. Bye for now.

Bye for now, I wrote.

On my way uptown to the Frick I realized I wasn't really dressed properly for an arts-world reception, but it was too late to go home and change. I untucked my shirt, hoping that made me look a bit more sophisticated, in an elegantly casual, GQ sort of way.

A girl about Gillian's age sat behind the check-in table in the entrance hall of the Frick. I could tell she had probably just graduated from Vassar or Sarah Lawrence and was thrilled with her new job as publicity assistant for some artsy publisher. This is another reason why I don't want to go to college: because I don't want to be someone who's just gotten out of college, smugly ensconced in their first "real job," wielding their nonexistent power and thinking they're going to be the editor of *Vogue* or *Vanity Fair* in a year or two. The Anna Wintour wannabe behind the table clearly had visions of corner offices, lunches at The Four Seasons, and photo shoots in Tangier dancing in her head.

"The museum is closed this evening," she said, smiling meanly at me. "This is a private reception."

"I know," I said. "That's what I am here for."

"Oh," she said. "Your name?"

I almost said James Sveck, but then remembered I wasn't and said, "Julian Braque."

She scanned her list down and up and then down again. She looked at me. "Did you say Julian Braque?"

"Yes," I said. "With a *B*. B-R-A-Q-U-E."

"I know how to spell Braque," she said, "and there's no Julian Braque here. There's a Philip Braque."

"That's me," I said. "Julian Philip Braque. The Third. I don't usually use my first name for business reasons. I get confused with my father, Julian Braque the Second."

"Wouldn't it be Junior?"

"What?"

"Your father's name. The second is a Junior, and the third is a Third, but there's no second."

"Of course," I said. "But my father has an aversion to being called Junior. He's a very large man."

"I'm sure he is," the girl said. "Well, Mr. Braque, you're down here as a guest of John Webster."

"Exactly," I said.

"Enjoy the reception," she said.

As soon as I entered the courtyard I saw John. He was standing next to the fountain at its center, talking to a woman I thought was my mother, but then I realized that practically all the women in the room resembled my mother—or, more accurately, she resembled them. They all wore sleeveless dresses exposing their tanned skin and big clunky necklaces made from coins and trinkets plundered from various ancient civilizations. The woman John was talking to had long maroon hennaed hair which she had pinned up in a deliberately messy way atop her head, and as she spoke with John she kept patting it and shoving the pins in and out. John was leaning slightly away from her as if she was perhaps spitting as she talked. He was sneaking peeks at his watch and glancing around the room, but the woman didn't seem to mind (or even sense) his obvious inattention. I stood against the wall beneath one of the arcades. A waiter passed by with a tray of champagne and I took a glass. When I looked back at John he was staring right at me. He looked startled and perplexed. I raised my glass, as if toasting him, and took a sip. He excused himself from the red-haired woman and approached me.

"James, what are you doing here?" he asked.

I was bothered by the demanding, almost censorious way he asked the question, as if I were a little boy who had invaded the grownups' party in my pajamas. "What do you mean?"

"Don't play games with me, James. What are you doing here? I know you weren't invited."

"How do you know that?"

"Were you invited?"

"Yes. In a manner of speaking."

"In what manner of speaking was that?"

"I was invited by a guest," I said.

"Who do you know here?"

I looked around the room hoping to spot someone I knew, or could possibly pretend to know, but except for the red-haired lady, who I felt I had a tenuous two-degrees-of-separation almost-connection with, there was no one. I looked back at John and said, "You."

"I know you know me, James. But who invited you?"

"You did," I said.

"I did not," said John.

"Yes you did," I said. I was aware of how childish I sounded.

He looked at me strangely for a moment, as if he had never seen me before. "I didn't invite you, James, I invited someone else, and if you'll excuse me I'll go see if he's here."

As he turned away from me I said, "He isn't here."

He turned back to me. "How do you know?"

"Well, he is here, in a manner of speaking—"

"Cut this crap, James, I don't think it's funny."

I looked around as if Philip Braque might actually be there, and I could point him out to John, and everything would be fine. But of course he wasn't. "It's me," I said.

"What do you mean?" John asked.

"Philip Braque is me."

"So it was you I was chatting with this afternoon?"

"Yes," I said.

John looked at me for a moment and then said, "Excuse me, James, but you're seriously fucked up. Fuck you." And then he turned and walked away into one of the side rooms.

He had spoken his final words so loudly that people standing nearby turned and looked at me. I didn't know what to do. I sipped my champagne, but my hand was shaking and I dribbled a little down the front of my shirt. I pretended I didn't notice. I felt very stupid standing there in my dribbled-on untucked shirt, which I realized looked stupid, not sophisticated, watched by all these elegant and successful people. I stood there for another moment so it wouldn't look as if I was running away, and when I thought I had established my equanimity I turned and walked across the courtyard and into the entrance hall. My friend was arranging rows of gift bags on the marble floor. "Don't forget your gift bag, Mr. Braque," she called out to me as I passed her and hurried out onto the sidewalk. I stood there for a moment, dazed, trying to figure out what had happened, but all I could think about was the fact that John had told me I was fucked up.

I heard someone say my name and I turned around. John was standing behind me. I saw that he had a gift bag and I absurdly thought, Oh, good—he can't be that angry if he took a gift bag. But he was angry. "Come with me," he said. He grabbed my arm just above my elbow and led me to the corner of Fifth Avenue, where we stood for a moment in silence. I thought maybe he was going to hail a taxi, but where would he take me? Was he going to take me somewhere and kill me? Then the light changed and we crossed the street. We walked uptown a block or two, and then he turned us into the park and steered us toward a bench, where he none-too-gently sat me down.

It was about seven, a beautiful summer evening, and the park was thick and green and lovely about us. I'm always shocked by the park—just the fact that it exists, this huge open space in the middle of the city. People strolled by or skated or ran past. Everyone seemed calm and happy.

We sat there for a few moments in silence. I was afraid to look at John, so I watched the people pass by. I think I thought that if I didn't look at him, he might not speak, that we might just sink forever into the idyllic stasis surrounding us. And then suddenly I couldn't stand the silence, the waiting for him to speak, so I said, "I'm sorry."

He didn't respond, just made a strange moaning sound. I looked at him. He was leaning forward, his elbows on his knees, his head in his hands. Was he crying? After a moment he said, "I'm very angry with you, James."

"I know," I said. "I'm sorry—"

"No," he said. "I don't think you understand. Listen to me." But he said nothing. An Irish setter trotted past us, pulling a man on Rollerblades behind him. "What you did was very mean, James. It was cruel. You can't fuck with people like that. It isn't funny. You obviously have no idea what it means for me to think I've met a smart and interesting man who is interested in me. It means a lot to me. There is nothing I want more than that. Nothing."

"I'm sorry," I said again.

"It was very cruel. If you were an adult, you would understand that. Did you think it was funny?"

"No," I said. "Well, yes in a way. I didn't think you would take it so seriously. I thought you would just think . . ."

"What?"

"I don't know. It was stupid, I know. But I thought you would be impressed. That I could create a person you liked."

"You don't think I like you?"

"I guess you do. But I don't mean like that. I thought you would like me more . . ."

"What do you mean?"

"I guess I was thinking that if I could create a person you liked, you would see that I am that person."

"But you're not that person. You're nothing like that person."

"I know," I said. "I guess I don't like who I am. I want to be that person. I wish I were that person."

"Well then, become that person. Learn about modern art and go study at the Sorbonne. But don't fuck around with other people."

I wanted to say I'm sorry again, but I knew it sounded so lame. But I said it anyway, because I didn't know what else to say.

We sat there for a moment in silence and then John stood up. "I'm going to walk over to the West Side," he said.

Because I didn't know why he was telling me this, I didn't know how to respond. "Okay," I said.

"I'm very sorry this happened. I'm very disappointed in you, James," he said. And then he turned and began to walk quickly away from me.

I didn't know what to do. I sat there until it got dark. It happened very slowly, almost imperceptibly. At some moment when it seemed that there was quite a bit of light still left in the sky the lamps along the pathways flickered on and after that it was difficult to tell the real light from the fake light. Or I suppose the light cast from the lamps was no less real than the light in the sky, but there was something false about it, and finally, after a long time, that was all the light there was.

12

Monday, July 28, 2003

WHEN I GOT HOME THERE WAS A MAN SITTING ON THE LIVING room couch, crying. He leaned forward, holding his head in his hands, covering his face, but I knew he was crying by the sound he made. For a moment I thought it must be my father, because I could think of no other man who would be crying in our apartment, but when I shut the door the man looked at me. It was Mr. Rogers. He resumed his hunched position and put his face back into his hands and cried for another thirty seconds or so, and then abruptly stopped, as if he were on a timer and had been shut off. He sat up straight, and looked at me again.

"What are you doing here?" I asked. I did not mean to sound interrogatory, but I did.

"Your mother asked me to come by and pick up my things," he said. "And leave my keys." He held up a set of keys, and jangled them at me.

"Oh," I said. "Well, she's not here now."

"I know. That's why I'm here, she wanted me to come when she wasn't here. She said she never wants to see me again."

I felt I was in no position to either refute or corroborate this statement, so I said nothing. But Mr. Rogers looked at me as if he expected a response.

"Well, do you need any help?" I asked.

"No," he said. "Unless you want to provide a shoulder to cry on."

I assumed he was making a joke, but he said it so sincerely I wasn't sure. So I tried to smile at him, in a way that suggested that I both felt sorry for him and found him funny. It must have looked weird because he said, "There's no need to look at me like that, James."

"I'm sorry," I said, and began walking toward the hallway.

"What did she tell you?" I heard him say.

I stopped walking but didn't turn around. "What?" I asked.

"What did your mother tell you?"

"About what?"

"What did she tell you happened to us in Las Vegas?"

I turned around and looked at him. "She told me you stole her credit and debit cards while she was sleeping and used them to spend or gamble away about three thousand dollars."

Mr. Rogers didn't say anything, he just looked at me as if he thought I would continue. And then when I suppose it became clear that I wouldn't, he said, "Legally, once we were married, the cards were joint property. Did she tell you anything else?"

"No," I said. "Did you do anything else?"

"Well, I did a lot of things," he said. "You spend a few days in Vegas with someone, you do a lot of things."

This was exactly the kind of moronic statement Mr. Rogers was given to making that had initially caused me to form my bad opinion of him.

"I meant did you do anything else that might have bothered my mother?"

"Apparently everything I do bothers your mother. I just wish she had decided that before she married me."

"But if she did, I doubt she would have married you."

"That was my point," he said.

"Well, maybe if you had stolen money from her before you got married, she would have decided that."

"I didn't steal it," Mr. Rogers said. "As I just explained to you, the money was ours. And in any case, I was borrowing it. I had every intention of giving it back. In fact, I was planning on winning big, and bringing her back more money."

"Well, I don't think that was a very good plan," I said.

"I know," he said. He leaned back into the sofa and then reached behind him and pulled out one of Miró's rawhide bones, which he likes to bury in the cushions. Mr. Rogers looked at it quizzically and then tossed it to the floor. He rubbed his hands together and sighed. "That's the sad thing. I knew it was a bad plan. Even while I was doing it, I knew. I mean, I told myself it would be great, I'd win big and I'd be happy and she'd be happy, and I'd take her to see those faggy lion tamers and we'd drink champagne and eat fish eggs, but of course I knew it was a mistake, a terrible mistake. But I did it anyway. That's the awful

thing about being addicted to something. Even while you're doing it and loving it you know it's wrong, and you know you're
weak, and you know you're probably ruining your life."

This speech took me by surprise, and I wasn't sure how to
respond. Mr. Rogers lowered his head into his hands again, but
made no sound. After a moment I said, "Do you mean caviar?" I
don't know why I said this. I just felt like I had to respond, and
that was the only response I could think of.

He looked up at me. "What?"

"You said you would eat fish eggs."

"Fish eggs are caviar," he said.

"I know," I said. "It's just that most people say caviar."

"Well, I say fish eggs," he said. "What's the big deal?"

"Nothing," I said.

"Do you think you're better than me because you say caviar?"
Mr. Rogers gave me a look that is usually described as "wither-
ing." "You never did like me, did you? You're a smug little bastard.
A smug little bastard who doesn't know shit." He pushed himself
up from the couch in an exaggeratedly old-mannish way, as if it
was all too much for him, and picked up a suitcase that was on
the floor. He gently placed it on the couch, and looked at it carefully, as if he might have the wrong suitcase. Then he patted it
fondly, as if it were his true love and he was rescuing it from the
awful world of our apartment. He looked over at me. "I left that
Nordic ski piece of crap in the bedroom. I can come back and get
it, or you can keep it. Or put it on the street. Throw it out the
window. Whatever you want."

In the early euphoric days of Mr. Rogers's and my mother's

romance, when apparently people think miracles can happen, he had bought a NordicTrack Skier and set it up in my mother's bedroom, where he intended to ski for twenty minutes every night before going to bed, and in this way restore his body to its former (supposed) glory.

"Don't worry," I said. "I'll deal with it."

"Then I suppose this is the end of the road for me," he said. He picked up the suitcase. "This particular road, at least."

I considered telling him that divorce proceedings and whatever criminal charges my mother might bring against him would prolong the road, but I didn't, because he looked so pitiable standing there with his suitcase, like the drawing of Willy Loman on the cover of *Death of a Salesman*.

"Well, goodbye," I said.

"Yes, exactly," he said. "Well, goodbye." He walked toward me, and for an awful moment I thought he was going to hug me, but he reached out and handed me the keys. Then he turned and went out the door.

I waited, listening to his footsteps descending the stairs and the *thunk thunk thunk* of his suitcase as it hit each railing, and then, when I was sure he was gone, I closed the door and locked it. I bolted it. I had a strange feeling that there was someone else in the apartment. I suppose it was opening the door and seeing Mr. Rogers sitting in the living room, but I felt like strange people might have occupied all the rooms, so I walked through the apartment, looking in every room. Of course, there was no one there except for Miró, who was sleeping on my mother's bed. He raised his head and looked at me uninterestedly, and then sighed judgmentally and resettled himself. I noticed there was a folded piece of paper lying on the floor by the bed, which I assumed Miró had displaced. I went over and picked it up, unfolded it. It was a note to my mother from Mr. Rogers, and I read it:

Dear Marjorie, I am so sad and disappointed. I'm sorry I have failed myself but I am a thousand times sorrier that I failed you. You do not know how sorry that makes me—to fail the person who gave me back my life. I hope you know that I will always love you. I am a stupid man so I don't know very much about forgiveness, but if you could find it in your heart to forgive me I know I would never disappoint you, or myself, again. Please give me that chance. Your devoted husband, Barry

I thought maybe I should throw it away. I knew the note would upset my mother, and since there was no way she would get back together with Mr. Rogers, what was the point of her reading it? He had already upset her once, why give him another chance? Then I thought about how in *Tess of the D'Urbervilles* Angel Clare doesn't find the note that Tess slips under his door because it slides beneath the rug and how basically because of that a lot of awful things happen and she ends up dead and so I decided not to interfere with the natural course of events.

I made myself a fried egg sandwich and ate the remaining third of a carton of Ben & Jerry's Cherry Garcia frozen yogurt that I found in the freezer and then went into my bedroom and did a search for three-bedroom, two-bath houses built before 1950 and under $200,000 in Indiana. There were lots and some of the houses were really beautiful. Made of stone, real stones that aren't identical, with screened porches and birdbaths in the front yards, front yards with big old trees rising above the house, trees that might be struck by lightning during a thunderstorm and collapse upon the house, but probably not.

A little after eleven I heard my mother and Gillian arrive home. They had gone to see *Long Day's Journey into Night*, an outing which was a present for Gillian's twenty-first birthday. Neither of them seemed to think that going to see a four-hour tragic play about the most dysfunctional dramatic family ever was an odd choice for a mother/daughter birthday celebration, but such are the dynamics of my family. My door was closed and my mother knocked softly on her way down the hall.

"What?" I said.

"Are you awake?"

"No," I said.

"Has Miró gone out?"

"No."

"Well, will you take him before you go to bed?"

"Yes," I said.

"Good night," she said. She sounded tired.

"How was the play?" I asked.

"Very good," she said. "But long. I'm exhausted. Good night."

"Mr. Rogers was here," I said.

"Oh," she said. "I told him to come by and collect his stuff. Did you see him?"

"Yes," I said. "He was here when I got home."

"Well, I'm sorry if that was awkward for you."

"It was fine," I said.

"Well, it's the last you'll see of him."

I didn't say anything because I thought, How do you know that? I could see him tomorrow on the street. Maybe you'll read his note and call him and he'll come over tonight.

"Well, good night," my mother said.

"Good night," I said.

A few minutes later Gillian knocked on my door and said, "Can I come in?"

I felt that what with John and Mr. Rogers and my mother I had had more than my share of human interaction that evening, so I said, "No. Go away," which of course did not deter her from entering.

She opened the door and walked into my room, looked around a moment, and then sat on my bed, as if she had only wanted to enter the room, not talk to me.

After a moment I said, "What do you want?"

"Mom told me to talk to you."

"About what?"

"What do you think? About your I'm-not-going-to-college-but-moving-to-the-Midwest nonsense."

"It isn't nonsense."

"Yes, James, it is. I have been instructed to come and tell you that it's nonsense. It is nonsense, James."

"Well, I don't care. One man's nonsense is another man's . . . sense."

"You're so wise, James. You should write a little book of aphorisms."

"Fuck you," I said.

Gillian said nothing for a moment, and then she said, "Seriously, James, I wish you'd get over all of this and just go to college."

"Why do you care if I go to college or not?"

"I don't, really. But Mom said if I convince you to go to college, she'll get Dad to buy me an Austin Mini Cooper convertible as a graduation present. So you see, if you'd just cooperate and stop being so silly, everyone would be happy: Mom would be happy, Dad would be happy, and I would be happy."

"What about me?"

"You would be happy, too. Or not happy, but no less happy than you are now. And honestly, James, I honestly think you *would* be happier. Just because you hated high school doesn't mean you'll hate college."

"I didn't hate high school."

"Well, you could have fooled me. Did I miss something? I don't remember you being voted Mr. Congeniality."

"Just because I didn't sleep around in high school doesn't mean I hated it."

"So I was popular in high school. We aren't talking about me, James. We're talking about you. I don't know what you're so scared of."

"I'm not scared of anything."

"Then what's the problem?"

"I'm not not going to college because I'm scared, I'm not going to college because I don't want to go to college."

"Yes, but why don't you want to go? If it's not about fear, what is it about?"

"It's about not wanting you to get a Mini Cooper convertible. That's what it's about."

"Very funny, James."

"It's true. The reason I'm not going to college is I don't want to participate in a world that involves such shameful finagling."

"Well, I hate to break it to you, James, but there's only one world. And it's full of shameless finaglers."

"I know," I said. "I'm not stupid."

"Then what are you? You're either stupid or scared."

"Yes, and you're either a moron or a termagant."

"Name-calling, James—the last resort of tiny minds."

"Well, you called me stupid or scared."

"Which are adjectives, which *describe* things. Versus nouns, which *name* things. Like *termagant*, which is, by the way, an unacceptably foul word because it only applies to women."

"Well, it applies to you," I said.

"I don't think we're making any progress," said Gillian.

"So why don't you go away and leave me alone?"

"That isn't like me, James. I think we both know I'm a stronger-willed person than you, and besides, I think I want a Mini Cooper more than you don't want to go to college, so if you weren't brain-dead, you would simply decide to go to college and save us all a lot of time and trouble."

"Well, even if I did decide to go to college, which is not going to happen, I would make sure that Mom knew the decision was entirely mine and had in no way been influenced by you, so you wouldn't get your stupid car."

Gillian said nothing. She stood up and began to walk around my room, looking at things, touching things. "You know," she said, "you might not believe this, but I was scared when I went to college. I think most people are, no matter how confident or popular. You're starting a whole new life in a way, which is scary. And I hated it at first. Do you remember that awful roommate I had, Julianna Schumski, who looked like Bozo the Clown and constantly farted? And everybody seemed retarded or from another planet—it was awful. But do I wish I had never gone to college? No."

"I am curiously unmoved by your little speech."

"How about this, then—you go to college, I get the Mini Cooper, and then you're free to drop out and go live in an igloo if you want."

"How about this: you shut up and leave me alone."

"You're so tiresome, James. Maybe it would be best for everyone if you did go and live in an igloo." She opened the door, but didn't leave, just stood in the doorway. "Did Rainer Maria call?"

"I don't know," I said. "The phone rang a few times, but I didn't pick it up."

"Why not?"

"Because I wasn't expecting any calls."

"Yes—no one ever calls you, do they?"

"Many are called, but few are chosen."

Gillian shook her head and left, closing the door. I waited a few minutes and then took Miró out for a walk. We ambled

slowly around the block and then sat on the front stoop. Miró
likes to sit on the top step and look down on the people and dogs
passing by. So do I, especially late on a summer night—it's like a
slow dark parade. A young man and woman walked past—a
handsome young man and pretty young woman, the man in a
seersucker suit and the woman in an old-fashioned summer
dress—and they were walking a bit apart from one another with
a space between them, and the man was looking straight ahead
and the woman had her arms crossed against her chest, hugging
herself, looking down at her feet, at her toes that peeked out the
open fronts of her shoes, and they both had the same gleefully
suppressed smile on their faces, and I knew that they were
freshly in love, perhaps they had fallen in love having dinner in
some restaurant with a garden or tables on the sidewalk, perhaps
they had not even kissed yet, and they walked apart because they
thought they had their whole lives to walk close together, touching, and wanted to anticipate the moment they touched for as
long as possible, and they passed by without noticing me and
Miró. Something about watching them made me sad. I think it
was too lovely: the summer night, the open-toed shoes, their
faces rapt with momentarily tamped-down joy. I felt I had wit-
nessed their happiest moment, the pinnacle, and they were already walking away from it, but they did not know it.

Miró always knows when I am sad. He put his paw on my
knee and softly whined. Perhaps it was merely his way of telling
me he wanted to go back inside and get his biscuit and go to bed,
but there was, nevertheless, a tenderness in the gesture that com-
forted me.

+   +   +

When I got in bed I could hear one of my mother's self-empowerment CDs playing, leaking out of her open window and into mine. I lay in bed and listened. A woman spoke serenely, without inflection or expression, and every sentence was punctuated by the sound of a gong:

The past does not control the future.

You can do more than you think you can do.

Love is never wasted.

Never stop learning.

Look for beauty.

You are cleansed by sleep and dreams.

You do not honor the suffering or sorrow of others by giving it power to defeat you.

Have faith in nature.

No one can do all the things that you can do.

Honor the strength and beauty of your body.

Be challenged by defeat.

Believe in what you love.

Doing good empowers you.

Open yourself to the love of others.

Re-create your life every day.

Everything is always changing. Nothing lasts.

After about ten minutes the voice stopped proclaiming, but the chime continued chiming. Each chime was quieter than the one before and the interval between chimes got longer and longer until there was no chime at all.

13

Tuesday, July 29, 2003

JOHN DID NOT COME TO WORK THE NEXT DAY. BY THE TIME I arrived at ten o'clock he had already left a message saying he felt "under the weather" and would be staying home. It was a sunny hot day, so I hoped that he had gone to the beach, but I worried that what had happened the night before might have something to do with his not being at work.

I felt very bad that I had alienated John.

My mother also failed to appear that morning, but there was nothing unusual about that. My mother had this notion that nothing of any importance ever happened before lunch, so that only the little people—assistants and such—worked in the morning.

I sometimes got spooked working alone in the gallery. Anyone could walk in off the street and often anyone did, and the problem was you had to be cordial and welcoming even if you instantly knew they were freaks. John told me that if anyone really seemed dangerous I should tell him or her that the gallery was closing early and escort them out and lock the door. If they refused to leave I was to call the building's security guard, but since he spent most of his time out on the sidewalk smoking and saying things like "Baby, baby, you don't look so happy, I can make you very happy, baby" to the women walking by, and since the elevator (if it was working) took about half an hour to reach the sixth floor, I knew I would be dead before any help arrived.

Since there was no one in the gallery and nothing to do, I decided to call the real estate agent for one of the houses in Indiana I had seen the night before. I knew it would be easier not to go to college if I had an alternative plan in place, because then it could be seen as a positive thing—I'd be doing something rather than *not* doing something. I went to realtor.com and searched for the listing. The brokers were a married couple named Jeanine and Art Breemer. There was a tiny photograph of them beside the photo of the house. Jeanine was seated and Art was standing behind her with his hands pushing down on her shoulders, as if she might pop up if he let go. She appeared to be a rather squat woman, smiling in a studied, somewhat maniacal fashion, and wearing what was obviously a wig. Art wore a powder blue sports coat over a white turtleneck and looked glum. A caption beneath the photo read: *The Breemers: Two Heads, Four Hands, One Heart.* Besides being anatomically incorrect, I couldn't see what that had to do with selling real estate.

I dialed their number, wondering which of them I hoped would answer. I didn't really want to talk to either. "You've reached the Breemers," a voice said. "This is Jeanine, how may I help you?"

I said, "I'm calling about a listing I saw on the Internet."

"Marvelous!" she said. "Which listing are you interested in?"

I told her the number and she said, "Is that the one on Crawdaddy Road? Yes—it is, and I'm not at all surprised. That house is just too lovely for words. Would you like to see it? I'd love to show it to you."

"Yes, I guess I would."

"Well, we'd better move fast, because I know it won't stay on the market for very long. How about two o'clock?"

"Today?"

"Yes. Or I could do it this evening, if that's better for you. I'd just love you to see it in the afternoon, though—it gets such wonderful light."

"Today doesn't really work for me," I said.

"Well, what about tomorrow? Any time would be fine."

"Actually the weekend would be better for me."

"All righty. Should we say Saturday, then? Two o'clock? How does that sound?"

"That sounds good," I said.

"Fine," she said. "And may I have your name?"

"James Sveck," I said.

"Nice to meet you, Mr. Sveck. Do you have any questions about the house I might answer now?"

"Well, I'm curious about the name of the town. Why is it called Edge?"

"Oh, you're not from Edge?"

"No," I said.

"Oh, where are you from?"

"I'm from New York."

"Oh—where in New York? My sister lives in Skaneateles."

"I'm from New York City."

"Oh my goodness—New York City! And you're interested in a house here in Edge?"

"Yes," I said, "I am. I plan to relocate."

"Well, I can't say I blame you. I don't know how anyone's still living in New York City. I think you'll just love Edge. It was voted the seventeenth-best small town in Indiana, you know. It beat out Carlisle and Muggerstown and many of those other hoity-toity places."

"So why is it called Edge?"

"Oh, don't worry about that," she said, and giggled.

This seemed an odd response to me, even coming from Jeanine. "I'm not worried about it—I'm just asking."

"Well, good," she said. "Because there's no need to worry. Who was it said, 'What's in a name? A rose is a rose is a rose'?"

"Mmmm—that would be Shakespeare," I said. "And Gertrude Stein."

"Oh, you're good!" she said. "I used to know all that—all that poetry stuff. You know that poem *Hiawatha*? I used to be able to recite that from memory. 'On the shores of Gitchygoomie . . . Where the buffalo did wander . . . lived a girl named Pocahontas . . .' Well, I forget the rest, but I knew it all. It's a lovely poem. Do you know it?"

"No," I said. "I don't."

"Well, I'll find my old poem book and read it to you when you get out here. I know you'll love it. It's chockablock with rhymes."

"That's all very reassuring," I said. "I'm still a bit concerned about the name, though."

"Well, I told you, it's nothing to worry about. It's perfectly safe here. Safer than New York City, I can tell you that. I think you should just come out here and take a look at that house. I'm sure you'll fall in love with it."

"I'm just curious about why the town is named Edge. I'd like to know that before I come all the way out there."

"Well, I don't have the faintest idea. Towns just have names. Why is New York called New York?"

"Actually, the British named it after York, a city in England. After the Dutch had already named it New Amsterdam."

"Well, there's an exception to every rule. But I don't think we're getting anywhere at all quibbling about such a silly matter. Tell you what—why don't you just come see the house, and if you don't fall in love with it, I'll eat my hat."

Even though I knew this was an idiomatic expression, for a moment I had a vision of Jeanine Breemer eating a hat. For some reason I pictured one of those transparent rain bonnets that fold up into a little packet. My grandmother always had one in her pocketbook, and when I was little I loved to take it out and open it and try to get it to fold back up. (I never could.) "I think I'll keep looking," I said.

"Oh, I just hate to see you pass up this opportunity, but I suppose you must suit yourself. Did you take the virtual tour?"

"Yes," I said.

"Most of the damage is merely cosmetic," she said.

"What damage?"

"Oh—I didn't mean damage. I just meant you'll want to paint and wallpaper. It's amazing what a lick of paint can do."

"Well, I think I'm going to pass on this one, but thanks very much."

"Seriously? You're not even going to look at it?"

"It just seems a long way to go to look at a house I'm really not interested in."

"Did somebody tell you about the transfer station? You know, it's not at all sure it will be moved to Crawdaddy Road."

"What's a transfer station?"

"It's where people bring their refuse."

"Do you mean a dump?" I asked.

"Lord, no. It will be much more than just a dump. There'll be a recycling center and a Kit and Kabooble."

"What's a Kit and Kadooble?"

"*Kabooble.* Well, it's this little shed where if you have say a blender or toaster or something like that that you don't want anymore, if it still works, or even if it's broken but you think someone else might be able to fix it or maybe use it for parts, or maybe use it for something else, like you might use the blender as a flowerpot or something—well, you put it in the Kit and Kabooble instead of throwing it in the dump and then someone else can come along and take it. It's just great. People have been known to furnish a house from the Kit and Kabooble. It would be so convenient for you with a new house—you could just pop over and grab up all the good stuff before anyone else had a chance!"

"Well, that does sound great, but I don't think I want to live next to a dump."

"Oh, you wouldn't be next to it—you'd be across the street. And they're going to build a beautification wall around it, so you won't even see it. At least not from downstairs. And of course that's where you'll be spending most of your time, since the second floor isn't heated."

"What's a beautification wall?" I asked.

"Well," she said. "It's a wall, a big tall wall, made of wood, I guess, or maybe concrete, but real pretty with maybe flowers or something painted on it. They let the school kids paint the beautification wall that hides Route 36 and it's as colorful as can be. It always cheers me up driving past. Oh, and there will be shrubs, too—I think there's a rule that there's got to be a shrub every ten feet, so you can see when all is said and done it will only add to your property value."

"Well, it's been nice talking to you and I appreciate all your help, but I really don't think I'm interested anymore." I said goodbye, and quickly hung up. I waited a moment, thinking she might call me back. I didn't want to be stalked by Jeanine Breemer. And then I felt very sorry for her. The only real estate agents I've ever known are women like Poppy Langworthy, a friend of my mother's, who sold several million-dollar apartments a year simply by showing them to people who could afford million-dollar apartments, of which there seemed to be an inexhaustible supply in New York City. I wondered when Jeanine's last sale was. She seemed a bit desperate. I hate dealing with anyone who works on commission. For a long time I never knew that this type of employment existed, and then when I was about ten I went with my father to a BMW dealership in New Jersey to buy a new car and the salesman that helped us was so aggressive he practically tackled my father when he said he was going to look around some and started walking toward the door. I remember I asked my father what was wrong with the man and my father told me nothing was wrong with him, he was just a shark; that in some jobs you had to be a shark, and everyone understood it, and it was okay. I asked my father if he was a shark and he said no, he was more like a vulture, he let other animals make the kill and dined on the remains. I was very unnerved by these revelations, and wanted to ask my father if there were jobs for lambs and rabbits, but somehow I knew I shouldn't ask that question. I thought maybe I'd become more aggressive as I aged, but that hasn't been the case, so actually this is a problem I'm still dealing with. I thought people in the art world might be lamb-y, but they're not. John's definitely a shark in his groovy, laid-back way and my mother can get very vulture-y at times. So this was another compelling reason to move away from New York City and find a means of supporting myself that did not involve savage instinctual behavior.

A woman had come in while I was chatting with Jeanine Breemer and was carefully studying each of the garbage cans. She had a little notepad and was copying information off the labels on the walls that identified each piece.

#21. Aluminum, paper, found objects, shattered rabbit skin glue,
felt-tip pen, beeswax, human hair. 24" × 30".

After a while she strolled over to the desk, incredibly nonchalantly, as if she were walking somewhere else and the reception desk just happened to be in her pathway.

"Oh," she said, "hello."

I said hello.

"Is there a catalog?" she asked.

I said there was not.

"There's no catalog?"

"Yes," I said, "there's no catalog."

"Why is there no catalog?"

"The artist does not believe in catalogs. He believes the work should speak for itself."

"Oh," she said. "How sweet: the garbage cans speak for themselves."

"Yes," I said.

"Do they speak to you?"

Of course I had to say yes. This is what happens when you involve yourself in certain professions: you are forced to proclaim that garbage cans speak to you.

"What do they say?" she asked.

"Well," I said, stalling for time. "Because they are individual pieces of art, each one says something different."

"What does that one say?" She pointed to the nearest garbage can.

As if it were painfully obvious, I very quickly said, "It says everything is garbage. Art especially. And of course if art is garbage, then so is everything else. Even the things we think of as holy are garbage. Everything is disposable. Nothing concrete is precious. Religion is filthy."

She took a step back from the desk, as if I might be as lunatic as I sounded. "That's a lot for one garbage can to say," she said.

"It's very potent work," I said.

"Well," she said, "that gives me a lot to think about. I'm Janice Orlofsky. I write for *Artforum*." She held out her hand.

I shook it and said, "I'm Bryce Canyon."

"You're quite passionate about art, aren't you, Bryce?"

"I suppose I am," I said.

My mother appeared at that moment in a particularly weird outfit: dark glasses, a jumpsuit with lots and lots of zippers and pockets, and new shoes that were really nothing more than a few strips of leather atop a towering spike heel. She seemed somewhat incapacitated by both the shoes and the shades, and tottered blindly across the gallery, bumping into a few garbage cans on her way. She passed us without acknowledgment and disappeared into her office.

I tried to think of a joke along the lines of "What do you get when you cross Helen Keller with an anorexic fighter pilot?" but before I could Janice said, "Was that Marjorie Dunfour?"

My instinct was to say no because I was sure that if my mother was a decent gallery owner she would have recognized Janice Orlofsky from *Artforum* and stopped and chatted with her, but I was feeling so confused by everything that had happened that morning—or actually everything that had happened in the past twenty-four hours (or everything that had happened in my life)—that I decided it just might be easier to tell the truth, so I said yes.

Janice opened her little notebook and wrote something (probably something cruel and damning about my mother), and then stuck it into her pocketbook, which was a *Hogan's Heroes* lunchbox circa 1970. Then she turned around and walked out, tossing something into one of the garbage cans on her way. (A receipt from Duane Reade for a "Sweet 'n Smooth Sugar Wax" kit. And she actually did review the show in *Artforum* [vol. XLII, no. 2]: "Unnamed Artist, Mixed Media. Dunfour & Associates Gallery, July 16–August 31, 2003. *When Is Garbage Just Garbage? When It Stinks.*)

That afternoon, at Dr. Adler's, I tried to think of some way to talk about what had happened the night before with John, and as I was trying to collect my thoughts, which apparently were uncollectable, Dr. Adler said, "You know, we've never talked about September 11."

This was totally odd and unnerving. As I've mentioned, Dr. Adler said little during our sessions, and rarely suggested a topic, or instigated an exchange. I looked at her to see if she would acknowledge in some way how uncharacteristically she was behaving, but of course she did not, merely smiled at me with her generic meaningless smile, and moved her head in a little bobbing way that indicated she was waiting for me to speak.

"There are a lot of days we haven't talked about."

She said nothing, and when it became clear I wasn't going to say anything else, she said, "Would you rather not talk about September 11?"

"I assume you mean September 11, 2001," I said.

"Yes," she said. "I do."

I said, "I wonder how long it took for people to begin referring to December 6 as Pearl Harbor Day. Or did they do it immediately? Was it like the next day, or the next week, that people were saying where were you on Pearl Harbor Day rather than where were you on December 6?"

"I believe Pearl Harbor Day is the seventh of December." She smiled slyly as she said this, unable to mask her joy in correcting me.

"Whatever," I said.

"Well," she said, "how would you like to refer to September 11?"

"I would prefer not to refer to it."

"Why is that?"

"It seems unfair that I have to explain why I don't want to refer to something you brought up that I have just said I don't want to refer to."

She said nothing in her stop-being-silly-I'm-not-going-to-encourage-you way. *Just ignore him and he'll go away,* my mother used to say to Gillian when we were young and I bugged her. *Just ignore him. All he wants is attention.* In retrospect there seems to be something almost cruel about that—to simultaneously acknowledge and refuse someone's desire for attention—especially a child's. *All he wants is attention,* as if it's bad to want attention, like wanting money or power or fame. Perhaps it's why I prefer to be ignored now; I've been warped in some irreversible way. Of course, I'm sure I've been warped in countless irreversible ways. It occurred to me that therapy is an ineffectual attempt to reverse the irreversible ways we have been warped; it's like futilely trying to untangle a big mess of untanglable knots.

"I really have nothing to say about September 11," I said.

"Nothing?"

"Yes," I said. "It really bugs me how people talk about it, everyone saying where they were, what they had seen, who they knew, as if any of that mattered. Or how like people in Ohio were getting grief counseling, as if it had happened to them."

"You don't think people were affected by what happened?"

"Yes, okay, maybe they were affected, but they weren't in one of the planes or they didn't jump out of the buildings, so I think they should just shut up about it."

"I don't really follow you," she said.

"Fine," I said, "don't follow me."

"But I'd like to understand your thought. What you're thinking. You went to Stuyvesant, didn't you?"

"I think you know I went to Stuyvesant."

"Yes, but sometimes, James, people can ask questions to which they know the answer. It's a socially acceptable practice."

"I just wish you'd ask me what you want to ask me rather than finagling me."

"Finagle—that's an interesting word."

"I don't really understand how one word can be any more interesting than another."

She paused for a moment and then said, "You went to Stuyvesant High School. Stuyvesant High School is very close to Ground Zero. Therefore, I assume your experience that day was particularly intense."

"I know this is going to make you think I'm just being deliberately belligerent, but I really hate that term."

"What term?"

"Ground Zero."

"Oh. Why is that?"

"It seems like a euphemism to me. Like something they'd say in a James Bond movie. And it made it a destination. Like, 'Let's go down to Ground Zero. Let's go to Rockefeller Center. Let's go to Yankee Stadium.' "

"How would you like to refer to it?"

"I don't know. The World Trade Center site. Where the World Trade Center was. 'Let's go down to where the World Trade Center was before terrorists flew a plane into it and caused it to collapse.' "

"Okay. Well, given that Stuyvesant was very near to the World Trade Center site, I imagine your experience of that day was intense."

"I think everyone's experience of that day was intense."

She shook her head sadly. "I would agree with you," she said. "But that wasn't the point I was making. You were across the street from the towers. I assume you saw everything that happened. I don't think that was everyone's experience."

We did see everything that happened from the windows of our classroom.

For a while I didn't say anything.

I was thinking about something I had read about in the newspaper a month or two after September 11, 2001. It concerned this woman that no one knew was missing. No one missed her. No one reported that she was missing. No family or friends. Her neighbors didn't notice. She was such a quiet person and lived such a lonely life that her absence affected no one. The only person who noticed was her manicurist. She had a standing appointment every week to have her nails done, and when she failed to show up and couldn't be reached, the manicurist called the police. They broke into her apartment. They found a bird, a parrot or something, dead in its cage, and of course no sign of her, only the newspaper for September 11 still open on her kitchen table. It took more than a month for anyone to figure out that she was missing, and if it weren't for the manicurist, no one might ever have known.

After a moment I said, "I'm thinking about the woman who died on September 11 who no one knew was missing. Did you read about her?"

"I don't think I did," said Dr. Adler.

I told her the story of the woman and she said she had heard of several people like that—people who had died but had not been missed. At least immediately. She asked me why I thought I was thinking about that woman.

It made me very sad, that question. Sad and defeated. Because I knew she knew why I was thinking about that woman— I was thinking about my own tendencies toward aloneness and I thought I could end up like that woman, with a bird perhaps, or a dog—probably a dog, I know birds are supposed to make good pets but I think there's something creepy about them—but alone with a life that didn't touch or overlap with anyone else's, a sort of hermetically sealed life. I knew Dr. Adler knew I thought this and just wanted me to say it—to "express" myself, because she thought that by articulating those thoughts I might transcend or purge myself of them—but what she didn't know was that the story of the woman who disappeared like that didn't make me sad, I didn't think it was tragic that she left the world without effect. I thought it was beautiful. To die like that, to disappear without a trace, to sink without disturbing the surface of the water, not even a telltale bubble rising to the surface, like sneaking out of a party so no one notices you're gone.

"What made you think of that woman?" Dr. Adler asked again.

"I don't know," I said. "She just came to mind."

Dr. Adler looked at me like well, yes, but *why* did she come to mind? And I felt it was okay to think about the lady with the parrot and not think about why I was thinking about her if I knew why I was thinking about her, and I wanted to tell Dr. Adler that by wanting those things to be explained she was missing something else. I thought, It's enough that I've thought that, I don't need to say it. I don't need to share it. Most people think things are not real unless they are spoken, that it's the uttering of something, not the thinking of it, that legitimizes it. I suppose this is why people always want other people to say "I love you." I think just the opposite—that thoughts are realest when thought, that expressing them distorts or dilutes them, that it is best for them to stay in the dark climate-controlled airport chapel of your mind, that if they're released into the air and light they will be affected in a way that alters them, like film accidentally exposed. And so instead of answering her question, I said, "I did something very wrong yesterday."

She looked a bit startled but managed to cover herself and said, "Oh—what?"

I told her what I had done with John, and how he had reacted.

She didn't say anything for a moment. I could tell she was still thinking about the parrot woman and September 11, and trying to figure out what the connection between that and John was, and what to ask me to get me to make some connection. This was the other thing that was beginning to bug me about therapy: how everything was supposed to be connected, and the more connections you could make the better you would be. It reminded me of one of those puzzle things you did in elementary school, where you drew lines between equal things in different columns and eventually you got too many lines and everything was connected to everything in a big tangled mess.

"Why do you think you did that?" she asked.

"I think I wanted to prove that I could be this other person. A person who would attract John. And I thought if I could conceive of that person and convince John that person existed, then in some way I would be that person. Or have the potential to be that person. I know it sounds stupid, but it made sense to me. I didn't realize I was misleading John."

"So you're interested in John?"

"What do you mean, interested?"

"I think you know what I mean."

I said nothing. I was thinking that I wished I hadn't brought this up and we were still talking about the lost lady.

"What did you want to happen last night with John?" she asked.

"I don't know," I said. "I don't really know what happens when two people who are interested in each other—or is it one another? I can never keep that straight."

"I don't think it matters," she said.

"Of course it matters," I said. "One is right and one is wrong and if you don't care enough to get it right, you're . . ."

"You're what?"

"You're failing the world. That it's little things like that, like using the language correctly, that keep the world functioning. I mean functioning well. That if we let go of those things, everything will collapse into chaos. Mistakes like that are like little chinks in the dam, and you think they don't matter, but they accumulate, your mistakes and everyone else's, and then they do matter."

"But sometimes there aren't rules. As in this case—I believe *each other* is usually used when referring to two people and *one another* is used when referring to more than two people, but I believe that is a custom, not a rule, that there is really no correct form."

"How do you know that?" I asked. I thought she might be making it up.

"English is my second language. When you study a new language, you learn things like that."

I hadn't known that English was Dr. Adler's second language. She must be German, I figured, but she had no accent, at least that I could discern. I always feel humbled by people who speak more than one language. I envy them. It seems with two (or more) vocabularies, you could not only say so much more and speak to so many more people, but also think more. I often feel like I want to think something but I can't find the language that coincides with the thought, so it remains felt, not thought. Sometimes I feel like I'm thinking in Swedish without knowing Swedish.

"You brought up your experience with John and then you changed the subject. Why do you think you did that?" Dr. Adler asked.

"I changed the subject?"

"It appeared to me you did. You started to talk about language. Word usage."

"Well, it's all related," I said, only because I didn't like being accused of changing the subject, which I had not done deliberately. Of course that fact holds little weight in a shrink's office, because they aren't really interested in the things you do deliberately.

"How are they related?"

How is misleading John Webster and causing a scene in the Frick Museum like proper word usage? It seemed like one of those impossible SAT questions where you can't even figure out what's being asked, let alone answer it. But then it suddenly made sense to me.

"They're both about the correct or proper way to do something. There is a correct and proper way to use words and there is a correct and proper way to behave with other people. And I behaved improperly with John and feel bad, so I compensate by obsessing with language, which is easier to control than behavior."

I was quite impressed with this answer, but Dr. Adler stared at me as if she were still waiting for me to respond. She looked a bit preoccupied, and I wondered if she had even heard me. I knew from experience this was a tactic she used to get me to continue, but I felt that because I had answered her question I deserved some sort of response. "What do you think of that?" I asked.

She didn't say anything, just shrugged her shoulders a little, as if she didn't think very much of it at all. Then she sat up a bit straighter and said, "I think you're very clever," but she said it in a way that made it clear she was really saying that I thought I was very clever. The meanness of this stung me, so I said nothing. I thought of the expression "He's too clever for his own good." When I was in second grade my teacher had written that in the comments section of my report card: *James sometimes has a tendency to be too clever for his own good.* It seemed like some sort of riddle to me, like black and white and red all over, and I asked my mother what it meant. She said it meant I talked too much.

After a moment of silence Dr. Adler said, "Well, that's all the time we have today."

14

Tuesday, July 29, 2003

I stopped at home for a pee and something to drink on the way back to the gallery. Miró was lying in the bathtub. He often lies there in the summer, because it's cool, I think. He opened his eyes and watched me judgmentally. I wondered for a moment if it was okay to urinate in front of a dog, and then realized how absurd that was, so I gave Miró a kind of fuck-you-you're-a-dog look. In private I'm often nasty to Miró. I say things to him like "You're just a dog. You don't have a passport or a Social Security number. You can't even open doors. You're totally at my mercy." Or "Get a haircut. Put on some shoes." I know he doesn't understand what I'm saying, but I think he suspects something's not quite right.

I looked in the refrigerator for something to drink, which you'd think would be a relatively easy thing to find, but since no one in my family ever really shops, it can be difficult. At that moment there was a carton of Tropicana orange juice with only a few drops left in it (since it was the rule that if you finished something, you were responsible for replacing it, the competition not to finish something was keen), a quart of 2 percent milk that was three days past its expiration date, three bottles of Peroni beer, a liter of caffeine-free diet Coke that I knew belonged to Rainer Maria, and some of that disgusting soy milk stuff that Gillian had bought months ago when she was going through a supposed lactose-intolerant phase.

And so I was running the faucet, waiting for the cold water to get from wherever distant place it was to our kitchen sink, when Gillian came in through the front door. She entered the kitchen and said, "What are you doing here?" as if I didn't live there and have just as much right to be there as she.

"Not that it's any of your business," I said, "but I'm on my way from therapy to the gallery."

"That all sounds very pleasant," said Gillian. "Meanwhile, I've had the worst fucking morning of my life." She opened the refrigerator and stared into it.

"What happened?"

"Do you really want to know?"

"Sure," I said.

"Please be sure, because there's lots of it and it sucks."

"I'm sure," I said.

"Okay. Well, first I had this date to meet Amanda Goshen at the Barneys Warehouse Sale at noon."

"Who's Amanda Goshen?"

"She's this sort-of friend from Barnard. She was in my memoir-writing class last semester."

"You were in a memoir-writing class? Barnard offers classes in memoir-writing?"

"Yes," said Gillian, "and stop interrupting. If you're going to question everything I say, forget it."

"Okay," I said. "I just think it's a bit odd to be writing your memoirs before you've even graduated from college."

"These days you're never too young to write your memoirs," said Gillian. "So shut up. Okay, first I'm walking along Bank Street past the brownstone that has that ridiculous miniature privet hedge growing in front of it and I'm just running my hand along the top of it, sort of patting it on its head as I walk past, and this lady appears from behind me and says, Don't touch the privet. And I can't believe this lady is telling me not to touch the privet. I mean, how sick is that? So I look at her and I say, What do you mean? and she says, I mean this is my privet, it's private property, and I wish you wouldn't manhandle it. She actually used that word, *manhandle*. And I swear I was barely touching it, you know, just running my hand along the top, tickling my palm, and I can't believe this woman is yelling at me for manhandling her privet, so I grab a handful of it and yank and throw it at her and say, Fuck you and your privet, and keep walking. And she's screaming after me that she's going to call the cops. And meanwhile there must have been thorns or something in the fucking privet because my palm is cut and bleeding. Just a little, but still. See . . ." She closed the refrigerator and displayed her palm, which had indeed been injured. "Okay, so you can imagine what kind of mood that puts me in, and I get to Barneys, and I'm waiting outside for Amanda and it's sunny and hot, so I'm leaning against the building and I'm wearing this tank top and I pull the straps down so I won't get lines, and an old man comes up to me and says hello in this very friendly way, as if he knew me. And I thought he was Mr. Berkowitz, so I say hello, very friendly, and then I realize it isn't Mr. Berkowitz but just some dirty old man that looks like Mr. Berkowitz. And I realize he thinks I'm a hooker or something because he asks me if I'd like to go on a date with him. A date, okay. He wants to take me somewhere and manhandle me and give me money and he calls it a date. So I say, No, I don't want a date, and he says, Why not, it looks like you're looking for a date, and I say, I'm not looking for a date, I'm just waiting for my friend, and he says, I'd love to watch you and your friend be friendly together—this is an old man who's a dead ringer for Mr. Berkowitz, remember—and I tell him to fuck off and he calls me a bitch and starts to walk away and then he turns around and spits at me, but he's not a very good spitter and it just sort of dribbles down his shirtfront, so he calls me bitch again and walks away. Okay, so by now it's like quarter past twelve and I'm still waiting for Amanda and I wait for another five minutes and my cell rings and of course it's Amanda and she says she can't meet me because guess what, she's sold her memoir to HarperCollins for $600,000 and she's having lunch with her editor in the Grill Room of The Four Seasons and if I see a pair of jade green Giuseppe Zanotti sandals would I buy them for her and she'll reimburse me? Okay, so at this point I decide I can't deal with the Barneys Warehouse Sale and I walk the ten blocks home and I think about buying an iced coffee and I think no, there's a bottle of Smartwater in the fridge and that's much healthier especially since you've already had three coffees, and I get home and of course the Smartwater has disappeared. Did you drink it?"

"No," I said.

"Then it must have been Mom."

"Do you think she was lying?"

"Who? Mom?"

"No. Amanda Goshen."

"About lunch at The Four Seasons?"

"No," I said. "About selling her memoir for $600,000. About selling her memoir, period."

"No, I'm sure it's true. She had the greatest memoir; she had all the best things wrong with her—incest, insanity, drug addiction, bulimia, alopecia: you name it. All the perfect stuff for a memoir. She's so lucky."

"What's alopecia?"

"Hair loss. She was bald, all over." She opened the refrigerator and gazed inside again, as if the bottle of Smartwater might have magically appeared. It had not. She closed it. "Oh," she said, "by the way, before I forget—Jordan Powell called you this morning."

"Who's Jordan Powell?"

"Your roommate."

At first I had no idea what she was talking about and then I remembered getting a big envelope from Brown a few days ago that I threw away without opening, since I thought opening and reading mail from Brown would only deepen my connection to it, the way if you open a box of cookies in a grocery store you are obligated to buy them.

"What's his name?"

"Jordan Powell. Or Howell. No, it's Powell, I think. I wrote it down somewhere. He's 'passing through New York on his way to the Vineyard,' and was hoping to get together with you. I told him you'd call him back tonight."

"Well, I won't," I said. "There's no reason to call him, since he won't be my roommate, since I'm not going to Brown. What did he sound like?"

"Like someone who would say 'I'm passing through New York on my way to the Vineyard.' But besides that he sounded okay."

I filled a glass with not even remotely cold water and drank it.

"Are you going out?" Gillian asked.

"Yes," I said. "I'm going back to work."

"Would you stop at Starbucks and get me an iced coffee? Please?"

"What, and bring it home to you in four hours?"

"No. Go to Starbucks, get the iced coffee, bring it back here, and then go to work."

"Maybe I could pick up your dry cleaning while I'm out there," I said.

"It wouldn't kill you to get me an iced coffee."

"No, but not getting killed doing something is not a very compelling reason to do it."

The gallery was empty (surprise!) when I returned and the door to my mother's office was closed. I sat down at the desk. It was two-thirty, which meant I had to sit there for another two and a half hours. My mother's gallery was in a building of galleries surrounded by other buildings of galleries, and I thought of how in most of those galleries there was someone like me, sitting alone in the air-conditioned chill with nothing to do except try to look as if there was something to do, and then I realized it probably wasn't just at galleries, that throughout the entire city thousands of offices must be sunk into this midsummer, midafternoon stupor. New York is strange in the summer. Life goes on as usual but it's not, it's like everyone is just pretending, as if everyone has been cast as the star in a movie about their life, so they're one step removed from it. And then in September it all gets normal again.

I got up and looked out the window and there was no one on the street, and there was something spooky about it. There are these strange moments in New York City when it seems as if everyone has disappeared. Sometimes I go out early on Sunday morning, and there's no one around, just stillness and quiet, or I'll wake late at night and look out the window and there will be no lights on anywhere, in all the apartment buildings surrounding us, and I'll think, Can it be possible that everyone is asleep? Is the city that never sleeps sleeping? Then someone appeared below me on the street: an old man walking a basset hound. The man walked very slowly, but the dog walked even slower. It was almost difficult to tell if they were moving. They reminded me of those sprinklers that follow a hose laid across the ground, rolling it up as they go. When I was young they really bothered me because they seemed to move without moving. I would spend hours watching, trying to see them move. I realize a child who spent hours watching a sprinkler not seem to move across a lawn was destined to grow up to be a disturbed person like me.

"James."

I turned around and saw my mother standing beside the reception desk. She was looking at me strangely, as if she hadn't seen me in a very long time. "What are you doing?" she asked.

"Looking out the window," I said.

"Oh." She seemed to consider this for a moment, as if it was a suspicious activity she had never heard of. She tapped her fingernails on the top of the marble counter and then said, "I'd like to talk to you. Why don't we go into my office?"

This seemed odd to me, since there was no one else in the gallery, so we hardly needed to go to her office for privacy. "Okay," I said, and followed her down the hall into her office. She sat down at her desk and I sat in one of the two Le Corbusier club chairs that faced it. It was a little weird that she was sitting behind her desk. It made it seem very businesslike and official, and that's not how I think of my mother.

She moved some things around on her desk and then she abruptly stopped and folded her hands together in front of her, like a news anchor after a commercial break. And she looked at me as if she were looking into a camera. Her face was composed and cheerful, but you could tell she was neither of those things. "I just spoke with John," she said.

"Oh," I said.

"He told me what happened last night. He's very upset, and I don't blame him."

"What did he tell you?" I asked.

"He told me what you did. That you concocted a profile on some Web site and contacted him."

"Actually, he contacted me," I said.

"He didn't contact you, James, because it wasn't your profile. And I want you to be quiet and listen to me." Her happy/composed look vanished and she looked at me in a scary/fierce way.

I said okay.

"John is very disconcerted by what you did. He doesn't want to come back to the gallery while you're here. He seriously threatened to quit. Fortunately, I talked him out of that."

"Good," I said.

"Yes," she said. "It is good. I'm sure you know how difficult things would be for me here if John left. It would be the end of the gallery. I can't replace him and I can't manage the gallery myself. And you may think this is all a game, James—the gallery and my life and John's life and your life—but they aren't. None of these things are a game. Well, maybe your life is, but that's for you to decide. Do you think your life is a game?"

"No," I said.

"Well, you seem to. Do you know what sexual harassment is?"

"Yes," I said, "of course I do."

"Then why did you do what you did? Didn't it occur to you that it was wrong? Illegal, in fact? That you're not supposed to put your co-workers in embarrassing sexual situations?"

"That's not what I thought I was doing," I said.

"Oh. What did you think you were doing?"

"It was just sort of a joke," I said.

"A joke? You think misleading someone and putting them in an embarrassing situation is a joke?"

"I didn't think that's what I was doing. Of course I wouldn't have done it if I thought that."

"Then what did you think you were doing? What could you possibly have been thinking?"

"I don't know," I said. "I guess I wasn't really thinking."

"Well, perhaps you might start thinking," my mother said. "And perhaps you might start thinking about someone other than yourself."

"I'm sorry," I said. "I apologized to John. I told him I was sorry. Didn't he tell you that?"

"Yes, he did," my mother said. "But sometimes that's not enough."

"Well, what else can I do?"

"There's very little you can do," my mother said. "At least now. So it was up to me to do something."

"What did you do?"

"I told John you wouldn't be working here anymore."

"You're going to fire me?"

"Well, I suppose I am, although I don't really like to think of it in that way."

"Oh," I said. "In what way do you want to think of it?"

"I don't think you should talk to me like that, James. Especially at this moment. I did what I did because of what you did. I think you should think about yourself, and not worry about me. Think about what you did."

"I don't see why it's such a big deal," I said.

"Well, perhaps that's why you need to think about it, because I assure you it is."

"Why? John is my friend."

"He's not your friend, James. He wasn't your friend before this and he certainly isn't your friend now. And it's actually worse if you thought he was your friend. That you would do something like this to someone you thought of as your friend."

I knew that my mother was wrong—John was my friend, or had been my friend. Maybe he didn't know he was my friend, and maybe I wasn't his friend, but he was my friend. And now he never wanted to see me again and probably hated me. I realized that it's very hard to like people, let alone love them—it just makes you do all the wrong, alienating things. "John was my friend," I said.

"Well, maybe he was," my mother said, "but I don't think he is anymore."

She said this in a smug, pleased way that really bugged me. Like because I had done something stupid in an effort to get close to somebody I deserved to be ostracized and ridiculed. It made me angry that my own mother welcomed my misfortune. I knew she thought it was probably good for me, a so-called learning experience. The problem is I don't ever learn anything from learning experiences. In fact, I make a special effort *not* to learn whatever it is the learning experience is supposed to teach me, because I can't think of anything drearier than being somebody whose character is formed by learning experiences.

"James," my mother said, "I've been wanting to talk to you about something and I haven't quite known how, but after what happened last night . . ."

"What?" I asked.

"Well, I've just wondered if perhaps . . . Are you gay?"

"Why does everyone keep asking me if I'm gay?"

"Who else has asked you?"

"Dad."

"Oh," she said. "Well, what did you tell him?"

"Why do you want to know what I told him?"

"I don't know," my mother said. "I suppose it was just another way of asking the question."

"Why would you ask me that question? Did you ask Gillian?"

"No," my mother said.

"Why not?"

"Because I didn't think Gillian was gay."

"So you think I'm gay?"

"I don't know—yes: the thought has occurred to me."

"But why would you want to know?"

"Why would I want to know? You're my son, James. I care about you. I want to help you."

"You think homosexuals need help?"

"James. Oh, James! I don't know what to do. I don't know

how to help you. I'm so worried about you, and I want to help you, but I don't know how."

I didn't say anything. My mother started to cry.

I knew she wanted to help me. I knew she was my mother and loved me and I didn't want to be mean, or I didn't think I wanted to be mean, but there was something else inside me, something hard and stubborn that was mean. It just bugged me that she thought if I was gay she could do something to help, like give me a Band-Aid or something. And besides, being gay is perfectly cool these days, so why should I need help? And what help could my mother, whose third marriage only lasted a matter of days, be? I knew I was gay, but I had never done anything gay and I didn't know if I ever would. I couldn't imagine it, I couldn't imagine doing anything intimate and sexual with another person, I could barely talk to other people, so how was I supposed to have sex with them? So I was only theoretically, potentially homosexual.

We heard the chime that signaled that someone had entered the gallery. "I think we should talk more about this," my mother said. "We can do that at home. And I think you should have a talk with your father. Now, since someone's come in, you can go back to work."

"What?" I asked. I couldn't believe that my mother could call me into her office, fire me, imply that I was a socially retarded loser, a sexual deviant, and then briskly tell me to go back to work. It pretty much contradicted my entire notion of who she was and how she felt about me. And then I realized I could not bear to hear her repeat what she had just said, so I got up and left her office before she had a chance to.

Whoever had walked into the gallery had already walked out, so I sat down at the reception desk, but it occurred to me that if you've been fired you don't go back to work, although just sitting there doing nothing, which is probably what I would do for the rest of the afternoon, isn't really working, but still. So I decided to walk out. Let someone come in and steal all the garbage cans if they wanted. Let my mother answer the phone in the rare event that it rang. I stood up and looked at the desk, searching for what I should take home with me. It always seems that in movies when people get fired they pack up all their personal belongings in a cardboard box which they carry for-lornly away with them. Usually there's a spindly plant, a THE WORLD'S BEST (fill in the blank) coffee mug, and a picture frame with photos of ugly beloved people. There were none of these things on my desk. Granted, I had only worked there for a few months, but it was kind of depressing to think that my tenure there had left not the slightest mark.

So I just walked out, down the hall, and waited for the eleva-tor, which of course was lost somewhere in space, and since I just wanted to get out of there I ran down the five flights of stairs and out onto the street.

I leaned against the wall outside the building, because I was panting from running down the stairs and had to catch my breath. The old man with the basset hound was walking toward

me. It seemed so long ago I had seen them walking on the opposite side of the street and I thought that time had moved differently in the gallery and on the street. I often have that feeling, a
sort of jet-lagged feeling just from moving from indoors to outdoors, or even from one room to another.

I stood there and watched the man and dog pass me by. I
didn't want to think about what had happened upstairs so I was
trying not to think. That was probably why I felt so spacey. Every
time I felt a thought forming I would think, *Don't think that. Don't
think that, don't think that. Don't think that.* It was like whacking a
lot of flies with a flyswatter. I don't know how long I stood there.
Long enough so that the man and dog walked all the way to the
end of the block and disappeared around the corner. And then I
realized I shouldn't stand in front of the building because my
mother might come out and I didn't want to see her. So I walked
over to the Hudson River promenade and sat down on a bench.
It was very hot and unpleasant. Sometimes you can sit on the
promenade and look out across the water and forget about the
city behind you and the ruined, ugly shore of New Jersey in front
of you, and just focus on the river, the light on the water or the
boats passing by, or the way, if the tide is rising, the water seems
to be going in both directions at once, the salt water pushing up
and the fresh water pouring down, but this wasn't one of those
times. I couldn't lose the sense of the city behind me and the
river didn't appear to be flowing in any direction, it just looked
stagnant and defeated. I stood up but I didn't know where to go.
I didn't want to go home because I knew Gillian would think it
was hilarious I got fired by my own mother. And I didn't really

want to see my father either, especially with his new eyes. I had already seen Dr. Adler and I had been a jerk with her and I wouldn't see her again until Thursday. And then I thought I'd like to see John, that he was the only sane, normal person I knew, but then I remembered I couldn't see John because of what I had done the night before, that I had fucked everything up with the one person I liked and that I'd probably never see him again and he would never think about me or if he did it would be to tell people about this weird pathetic boy who had stalked him.

15

Tuesday, July 29, 2003

Even though it was only four o'clock, Grand Central was crowded and everyone was running and pushing to get on their trains so they could get out of the city. It was like some mass evacuation at the end of the world, everyone fleeing in this exhausted way from one miserable life to another. You could tell they hated their office lives but weren't exactly looking forward to returning to their irritable spouses or bratty children, or to no one, if they were alone. The train ride was this little hiatus between two parts of their lives during which they could simply be themselves, no boss, no wife, no colleagues, no children.

The woman I sat beside read the Bible. She had one of those laminated religious bookmarks with a gory picture of Jesus and a little pink tassel and she used it to follow the text from one line to the next. She moved her lips and very softly uttered each word while she read. There was something about the juxtaposition of the bleeding Jesus with the pretty pink tassel that unnerved me. It was like putting a severed heart into a box and covering it with pretty wrapping paper. When she got off (at Woodlawn) she kissed the bookmark and then closed it into the Bible. Sometimes I envy religious people for the comfort of believing. It would make everything so much easier.

I walked from the train station to my grandmother's house, through the residential streets with nice old houses and big trees and green lawns. A team of Mexican gardeners worked at one house, and a boy who I could tell was younger than I was pushing a lawnmower almost as big as he was across the lawn. He looked at me and smiled as I walked past, smiled in a very happy, friendly way, exposing his beautiful white teeth, as if he was proud of being seen mowing the lawn. I smiled at him, and he waved. It's odd to connect with people like that and then just walk away. I don't get it. And it's weird because I'm antisocial, but when I connect with a stranger—even if it is only exchanging smiles, or waves, which I suppose isn't really connecting, but for me it is—I feel like we can't both go on with our lives as if nothing had happened. For instance, the Mexican boy, cutting a lawn in Hartsdale, how did he get there, where did he live, what was he thinking? It's like there's this pyramid of his life, an iceberg, and I just see the tip of it, the tiny tip, but it spreads out beneath that, spreads out and back and back, his entire life beneath him, inside him, everything that ever happened to him, all adding up to equal the moment, the second, he smiled at me. I thought of the lady beside me on the train reading the Bible. Where was she now? In her home? I know I shouldn't have gotten off the train at

Woodlawn and followed her home, but what if I should have? What if she was meant to be, or could have been, someone important in my life? I think that's what scares me: the randomness of everything. That the people who could be important to you might just pass you by. Or you pass them by. How did you know? Should I turn around and talk to the Mexican boy? Maybe he was lonely like me, maybe he read Denton Welch. I felt that by walking away I was abandoning him, that I spent my entire life, day after day, abandoning people.

I realize it makes no sense to feel that and yet never make any attempt to interact with people, but I am beginning to think life is full of these tragic incongruities.

It was eerily quiet and still on my grandmother's street. She lives in the kind of neighborhood where the kids are too rich and privileged to do something as simple as play outdoors. They were all at their violin or judo lessons or had been packed off to equestrian or theater camps. The only animate things were the sprinklers, the clapping spigoty kind, spewing shimmering jets of water low over the perfectly green lawns. The sidewalks were old and made of separate plates of concrete, which were cracked by tree roots and the constant shifting of the earth. They were warm and dusty. I thought about the sidewalks in the city, about how mostly gross they were, how you would never want to lie down and rest your cheek on them. But the sidewalks on my grandmother's street were different, they were like the ruins of ancient Rome, purified and ennobled by time, baked clean by the sun.

The front door to my grandmother's house was closed. I

knocked, but there was no answer, so I went around to the back. On the porch table sat an empty mug of coffee and a half-smoked cigarette smashed out in a lopsided ashtray Gillian had made at a tender, talentless age (not that she ever became a talented ceramicist at a later age). My grandmother used to smoke a lot, but now she only smoked a couple of cigarettes a day: one in the morning, after breakfast, and one in the evening, after dinner. Always out on the porch. There was a bright scarlet smudge of lipstick on the rim of the coffee mug, and I liked the idea that my grandmother put on lipstick first thing in the morning, even though she might see no one all day.

I looked through the screen door into the kitchen. She wasn't there, but the radio was on (*All Things Considered*), so I went into the kitchen and called her. I knew if the radio was on, she must be in the house because she would never go out and leave it on. She had a hearing aid, but she rarely wore it, especially if no one was around.

She didn't seem to be downstairs, so I went upstairs. The door to her bedroom was open, and I looked in and saw her lying on the bed, on her stomach, with her arms and legs sort of flung out toward the four corners. It looked as though she had been dropped on the bed from a great height. I knew my grandmother would never sleep like that; there was something scary about it. Her face was turned toward me, the lower half mashed into the bedspread, and it looked as if she had been drooling. I thought she was dead.

Everything stopped for a moment, as if someone had hit PAUSE. And then I heard her snore, and I knew she was not dead.

I entered the room and stood close to the bed and said Nanette, but she did not wake. I could see her eyes moving beneath her nearly translucent eyelids. I worry sometimes about her skin—on the backs of her hands, her eyelids—it seems as if it's been worn to an almost unbearable thinness, like fabric damaged by too much time and light. I wondered what she was dreaming. If it was a good dream I did not want to wake her from it. So I sat down in one of the antique straight-back chairs on either side of her bureau.

The soft summer evening light seeped through the trees around the house and fell in golden swaths through the bedroom window. I could hear the clackety thrum of the sprinkler next door. And a bee trapped inside the screen window, buzzing and hurling itself softly against the mesh, again and again, as if it had all the time in the world, as if it might, at some moment, find a hole in the screen and fly away. I thought how patient and trusting so many lower forms of life are, how they had faith in something beyond human comprehension.

I sat there for about an hour. I might have fallen asleep myself, but I don't think I did. I just kind of zoned out, forgot who and where and what I was. Just let everything go, turned the net of myself inside out and let all the worried desperate fish swim away.

And then I heard my grandmother say, "James."

I looked at her. It had grown dim in the room, but I could see her face, still pressed against the coverlet. Her eyes were open, watching me.

"Yes," I said.

She looked at me for a moment with no expression, as if I was always there when she woke from a nap. Then she sat up. She patted her hair and dragged the back of her hand across her mouth, wiping away the drool. There was something uncharacteristically coarse about this gesture.

"What time is it?" she asked.

"I don't know," I said.

She looked around the room for a moment, as if to orient herself. Then she stood up and gently clapped her hands. "Well, I'm sure it must be time for a drink. Why don't you go downstairs and make me one, and let me attempt a reconfiguration. There is nothing uglier than an old lady woken from a nap."

Downstairs, I made her drink—rye and water on the rocks— and poured some assorted nuts from a tin into a little ceramic bowl that had the castle at Heidelberg painted inside it (I knew this because beneath the painting it said *The Castle at Heidelberg, 1928*) and put a record called *The Fountains of Rome*, which my grandmother thinks is "lovely cocktail music," on her old cabinet stereo and sat down and waited.

After a few minutes I heard her coming down the stairs. She entered the living room and I saw that she had changed her dress—she was now wearing a cream-colored, short-sleeved dress covered with big pink and blue hydrangea blossoms. And she had fixed her hair and face and put on some lipstick that matched the pink flowers on her dress. She saw the drink waiting for her on the coffee table and said, "Doesn't that look delicious." She sat down and said, "And I see you've made one for yourself, how smart you are." Then she raised her glass and said, "We're alive." This is a toast my grandmother often makes, but it means different things at different times: sometimes it means *Well, at least we aren't dead,* and sometimes it means *Isn't it wonderful we're alive!* I wasn't sure how it was meant this evening. I leaned forward and touched my glass to hers and said, "Yes, we're alive."

She sipped her drink and then said, "And it tastes as good as it looks."

I sipped my drink. I didn't really like it. I don't like drinking alcohol very much: it tends to make me sad and tired. Or sadder and more tired than I usually am. I always wait to get that happy funny feeling that supposedly comes with inebriation, but it never arrives. So I had made my drink much weaker than hers.

"So," she said. She opened a box of silver coasters and removed two. She put one down in front of each of us and then placed her drink onto hers. "So," she said, "to what do I owe this great pleasure?"

"What pleasure?"

"The pleasure of a visit from you."

"Can't I just come visit you?"

"Mayn't I. Yes, you may. Of course you may."

"Actually . . ." I said, but faltered. I didn't know how to continue. It seemed exhausting, to try to tell someone what was wrong with you. I remembered the Mexican gardener who smiled at me, and how I had thought about the pyramid beneath him, and it felt like that—that no one could understand who you were at a particular moment unless they understood the pyramid beneath you, and my grandmother probably knew me better than just about anyone in the world (including my mother), but it still felt impossible to tell her what was wrong. So I lowered my face and said nothing.

Most people would have said something, prompted me, but my grandmother didn't. She took another sip from her drink and then replaced it on the coaster, and then moved the coaster a few inches, as if it had been in the wrong place. And then she sat looking at it, as if it might move itself back. After a moment she reached over and put her hand on my knee and said, "Is something wrong?"

"Yes," I said.

"That's too bad," she said. She waited for me to say something, and when I didn't she leaned back into her chair. "Would you like to tell me about it?"

"Yes," I said, "but I don't think I can. I'm not sure what it is. It's not just one thing. It's everything."

"Everything," she said, confirming rather than questioning.

"It seems like everything," I said.

"Well, perhaps there's one thing, one part of it, you could tell me about. What is it that made you come out here?"

"There was nowhere else I could go. Or wanted to go." I realized that sounded terrible, like I was there as a last resort. But in a way that was true. I felt bad.

"Well, you're always welcome here," my grandmother said. "We can just sit and listen to the music if you'd like. Are you hungry? Would you like some nuts?" She picked up the bowl and held it out to me.

"No, thank you," I said.

She put them back on the table and then adjusted them, as she had her drink. My grandmother spent a good part of her life adjusting things, moving objects a few inches this way or that, as if there were a perfect place for everything.

We listened to the music for a minute or two and then she said, abruptly, "I don't want you to get the wrong idea. I don't usually take a nap. I never have. You see, my father wouldn't tolerate naps. He thought they were bad for you, and bad for commerce. Bad for the nation. He did a lot of business overseas, and the offices in Italy and Spain closed in the afternoon, everyone went home and took naps. Siestas. Or did something much worse, even wickeder than napping, I'm sure he suspected. It infuriated him. He was a real curmudgeon and didn't trust people who enjoyed life too much. That wasn't the point, as far as he was concerned. I remember once I came home from a party and was gushing about something I ate—I think there had been a lobster Newburg, or something exotic like that—and he told me it wasn't polite to talk about food like that. That it wasn't as good as all that and if it *was* that good there was something wrong with it. We always had very plain food at home. He wouldn't eat anything that had a foreign name. And he wouldn't put gravies or sauces on his meat because he thought it was decadent. Imagine—gravy! He tried to stop us from using gravy, too, but my mother wouldn't allow it. He let her be soft with us, but he pretended it disgusted him. Perhaps it did.

"So I don't usually nap. I still feel guilty when I do. But I was sitting out on the porch this afternoon reading a magazine and I must have fallen asleep, because I woke and felt so strange. I didn't know where I was. It took a minute, and then it all came back, but I still felt tired. So I thought, I'll just lie down for a few minutes, and I went upstairs. That was about three o'clock. And now"—she looked at her watch—"now it's six-thirty. I must be getting old."

"How do you feel now? Are you still tired?"

"No," she said, but in a tired way. And she looked tired, too. As if she knew what I was thinking, she said, "I'm feeling as fit as a fiddle. Although why fiddles are fit I know not." She paused and smiled at me. I noticed that her pink smile didn't quite match her lips. I looked down into my drink. My grandmother was going on about the fitness of fiddles, but I wasn't really listening. And then I realized she had stopped talking, so I looked up at her. She stared at me for a moment and then said, "Oh, James. Why don't you tell me what's wrong?"

I didn't know where to start. Maybe it was the rye—I had already finished my drink—but I suddenly felt warm and happy. I still believed that everything was wrong, but I didn't really care. It was like I was looking down on myself from the moon and could see how tiny I was and how tiny and stupid my problems were. So I had been fired, so I had acted like a jerk and alienated John, so I was a loner/loser, and so I didn't want to go to college. None of that really mattered. It wasn't like I was on a plane that had been hijacked and was flying toward the World Trade Center.

"I got fired today," I said.

"Fired?"

"Yes. From my job at the gallery. By my mother."

"And why did she do that?"

I told her what had happened with John. My grandmother sipped her drink while I spoke, and when I had finished she held out her glass to me and said, "I think we both need another drink before we continue. You go make them and I'll turn the record over."

We followed her plan and in a few minutes we had resumed our places, our drinks were fresh, and the B side of *The Fountains of Rome* was playing.

"You know," my grandmother said, after she had tasted her new drink and made a noise indicating that she approved of it, "I think it's rather a heartening story, what you told me. You acted stupidly and made a mess, but nevertheless I find it heartening."

"Why?" I asked.

"Why? Because you wanted something, and tried to get it. You *acted*. You acted stupidly, but you acted, and that's the important part. And people often act stupidly when it comes to love. I know I did." She paused for a moment, as if she was remembering something specific.

I was shocked. She had said "love," had mentioned love as if it was an element of the story. I thought for a moment that I had misheard her. I've never talked about being gay or straight or anything remotely connected to that with my grandmother. It was like she lived in this other world, the world of Hartsdale, the world of men who wouldn't even put gravy on their meat, a world where those things didn't exist. Did she think I loved John?

"Are you listening, James?" I heard her say.

"Yes," I said.

"You didn't look as if you were," she said. "Well, in any case I don't think there's anything to worry about—it hardly matters to be fired by your mother from your mother's business; it's like being sent to your room when you're naughty, and nothing more than that. And if this John fellow is a human being, he'll realize that what you did, while stupid, is actually flattering and rather sweet—sweet in a dim, stupid way. But you've got to start somewhere."

"You don't think he'll hate me forever?"

"Goodness, no. A week or two, perhaps, but forever? Hardly. If he's got half a sense of humor about him, perhaps in time he'll even be flattered, as of course he should be. You might send him a note—a polite note of apology, and leave it at that. All one can do in situations like this is apologize, and then the ball is in the other court, so to speak."

She stood up. "I have lamb chops from the good butcher. And zucchini from the Takahashis' garden. I assume you're spending the night. Are you?"

"Yes," I said, "if that's okay."

"Of course it's okay. It's delightful. Should you telephone your mother? Does she know you're here?"

I lied and said yes. I knew it was bad not to let my mother know where I was, but I felt like since she fired me she didn't really deserve to know.

"Fine," said my grandmother. "So are all our problems

solved?" This, like "We're alive," is a catchphrase of my grandmother's. She's a great believer in solving all problems before sitting down to a meal or going to bed.

"Well," I said, "there's still the problem of college."

"I thought we solved that problem last week."

"Not really," I said.

"Remind me, what was the problem?"

"I don't want to go to college."

"Well, that seems very easily solved—don't go to college."

"I don't think I can," I said.

"You don't think you can not go to college? I'm not sure I understand you."

"Of course I could not go. The problem is what do I do if I
don't go to college."

"Well, that seems like a different problem entirely," said my
grandmother.

"Yes," I said. "I suppose it is. I wanted to use the money from
college to buy a house in the Midwest and move there, but now
I'm not so sure."

"That sounds like a rather dreary proposition. Remind me,
why don't you want to go to college?"

"I told you—I don't want to spend all that time in that environment with that kind of people."

"What kind of people?"

"The kind of people who go to college. People my age."

"Well, are there adult-school colleges? Or perhaps you could
go to a correspondence school. Although I suppose one doesn't
go to a correspondence school—that's the point. You could—

well, correspond with a correspondence school. Do you think Brown would let you correspond?"

"I doubt it," I said.

"I remember I saw an advertisement for a correspondence course in dog grooming—I think it was in the *Ladies' Home Journal*. Would something like that interest you?"

"Actually, I wouldn't mind grooming dogs. I like dogs. But I don't think my parents would approve."

"Well, James, you can't spend your entire life pleasing your parents. And there's really no pleasing your mother, is there? She fired you, after all."

"Yes," I said, "that's true."

"Well, why don't we have dinner, and then sort this out. I can never think straight when I'm feeling peckish. Are you hungry?"

"Yes," I said. I realized I hadn't had anything to eat all day. I had planned to eat something when I stopped at home after seeing Dr. Adler, but was thwarted by the empty refrigerator (and Gillian).

After dinner we played Scrabble (my grandmother won) and then, while I did the dishes, she smoked a cigarette on the back porch. My grandmother has a dishwasher but she never seems to use it. I don't think she trusts it—she only believes the dishes are clean if she washes them herself. When I finished with the dishes, I sat at the table and looked out the window, into the backyard. My grandmother was standing in the center of the lawn, smoking her cigarette. She had her back to me, so I could not see her face. It appeared as though she was studying something in the neighbors' yard, or perhaps she could see into their lighted windows. I remembered watching the spooky family through the window the night I escaped from the dinner theater, and for a moment I felt a little disoriented, like when you look into two facing mirrors, and the world opens up and collapses at either end. I was looking through a window at my grandmother, and she was looking through a window (maybe) at her neighbors, and maybe they were looking out their front windows at someone in the house across the street or in a car parked in front of their house, and on and on all the way around the world. As I watched, my grandmother raised her arm, brought the cigarette to her mouth, inhaled, and then released the smoke in a long exhalation. When she was finished, she stubbed the cigarette out in an ashtray she held in the other hand—the lopsided one that Gillian had made. I waited for her to turn around and come back into the house, but she remained standing like that, transfixed, it seemed, by whatever she was watching. So I went upstairs to put sheets on the bed in the guest room.

After a few minutes I heard my grandmother come inside and she did something in the kitchen (probably reclean the counters I had already cleaned) and then she came upstairs. I was sitting on one of the twin beds in the guest room, looking at a *National Geographic* magazine I had pulled from the pile on the nightstand. It was from 1964, and on the cover a white horse stood on its hind legs. The banner read: "Vienna's Very Own: Those Dancing White Stallions."

My grandmother stood in the doorway. "Thank you for cleaning up the kitchen," she said.

"You're welcome," I said. "Thanks for the nice dinner."

"I know we haven't solved the college problem, but—well—I don't think I can be much help to you with that. I don't understand enough how all that works these days. But I'm sure there are options for you, James. I'm sure it will all work itself out."

"Yes," I said. "I suppose it will."

"And if college is all wrong for you, if you really don't like it in the way you fear, well—it won't be a waste to have gone. Having bad experiences sometimes helps; it makes it clearer what it is you *should* be doing. I know that sounds very Pollyannaish but it's true. People who have had only good experiences aren't very interesting. They may be content, and happy after a fashion, but they aren't very deep. It may seem a misfortune now, and it makes things difficult, but well—it's easy to feel all the happy, simple stuff. Not that happiness is necessarily simple. But I don't think you're going to have a life like that, and I think you'll be the better for it. The difficult thing is to not be overwhelmed by the bad patches. You mustn't let them defeat you. You must see them as a gift—a cruel gift, but a gift nonetheless.

"I know I'm rambling, and I'll stop. I've felt queer today, ever since I woke up from that nap. But there is something else I want to tell you. Something I want you to know, now. It's about my will, James. I'm leaving everything in the house to you. The house itself will be sold, but everything in it will be yours. And I want you to do whatever you like with it all—keep it, sell it, give it away, burn it in a pyre, or any combination thereof. And of course you'll be getting some money, too, but that's too dreary to talk about."

I didn't say anything. I didn't know what to say. I was looking at a page of illustrations in the *National Geographic*, all pictures of white stallions doing different tricks.

"I just wanted you to know that," my grandmother said. "I
wanted you to know that it's important to me that you decide
what's to become of all my things."

"I'll keep them," I said. "I'll keep everything." I held up the
magazine. "I'll keep this."

"No," my grandmother said. "That's not what I want. They're
only things. They don't mean anything. Keep only what you
want." She walked across the room and kissed me, and stroked
my hair. "And now I'm going to bed," she said. "I don't know how
I can be tired after that long nap, but I am. And you look tired,
too."

"I am," I said.

"It's been a long day," she said.

"Yes," I said.

"Sleep well," she said.

"Yes," I said. "You too. Good night."

She said good night and left the room. I sat on the bed for a
while, thumbing through the magazine, but not really looking
at anything. I was thinking about all the things in my grandmother's house, and how much I loved them all. I felt in some
stupid way that if I kept those things near me, perhaps my life
wouldn't be miserable.

But I knew they didn't have that power, or any power at all.
They were only things. Objects.

16

Wednesday, July 30, 2003

I WOKE UP ABOUT NINE THE NEXT MORNING. FOR A MOMENT I wasn't sure where I was and then I recognized the curtains and remembered.

I found my grandmother in the kitchen. She had a huge mound of seriously deformed zucchini piled on the counter and was furiously chopping the long green tubes into disks.

"Wow," I said. "I feel sorry for those zucchinis."

"I don't," she said. "I hate zucchini. Mrs. Takahashi won't stop bringing them over. I always thought her English was quite good, but apparently she doesn't understand the meaning of 'Thank you, but no more zucchini.' So I'm making zucchini bread. I know it sounds awful, but it's quite edible. Would you like some eggs? I'd gladly leave these alone for a while and cook you an egg."

"No, thanks," I said. "I'm going to head back to the city."

"With no breakfast? How about some coffee?"

"I'll pick some up on my way," I said. I was eager to get home because I didn't want my mother to flip out and call the police or anything. I had sort of promised her after what happened in D.C. that I would never disappear like that again. "It was good to see you," I said. "I'll talk to you soon."

"It was good to see you, too," she said. She put down the knife and wiped her hands on her apron. "I'm sorry if I was odd last night. I'm feeling much more myself this morning."

"You weren't odd at all," I said. "You gave me a lot of good advice."

"I seriously doubt that," she said. "Go. You can catch the 9:57 if you hurry." She kissed me, and then pushed me away.

The train was pretty empty, just a gaggle of Bronxville soccer moms going into the city to spend money. There was something creepily alike about all of them, as if they were the same model of car, just different years: one wore a white sundress with pink stripes, another wore a pink sundress with green polka dots. They all wore sandals and had designer sunglasses perched atop their similarly coiffed heads. I found this spectacle somewhat depressing, because I had always thought, or hoped, that adults weren't necessarily as hobbled by mindless conformity as so many of my peers seem to be. I always looked forward to being an adult, because I thought the adult world was, well—adult. That adults weren't cliquey or nasty, that the whole notion of being cool, or in, or popular would cease to be the arbiter of all things social, but I was beginning to realize that the adult world was as nonsensically brutal and socially perilous as the kingdom of childhood. But beneath their gloss of confidence and entitlement, I could tell the ladies were nervous, almost scared, for they knew they didn't belong in the city anymore—once they married the investment banker and moved to Bronxville they ceased to be New Yorkers. The city is cruel in that way.

And then I thought that if I moved to Indiana (although after my conversation with Jeanine Breemer, I was having second thoughts about Indiana) I would be similarly exiled. I would be able to come back to the city, but I'd feel displaced like the soccer moms. Even if I went to Brown and came home fairly regularly, I might feel that way. Everything is always changing so quickly in New York City; if you go away for even a week you realize it: the Greek restaurant becomes an Ethiopian restaurant. The bakery has been transformed into yet another nail salon. I would be one of those people who emerged from the subway and looked around confusedly, having lost their sense of east and west, uptown and downtown. I'd start walking the wrong way, and have to stop and orient myself, like a tourist.

All this made me think maybe I should just stay and go to college here, and forget all about the Midwest and Providence, Rhode Island. I remember once in second grade the teacher pulled down the wall map of the United States and asked us to name the biggest and smallest states. Alaska was easy, but nobody guessed Rhode Island because it was so small you could barely see it. It was so small its name had to be written out in the Atlantic Ocean with an arrow pointing west. How could I move from the largest city in the country to the smallest state? Yet I

didn't know how I could go to college in New York, because I had
applied to and been rejected by Columbia (although they referred
to it as "not being able to find space for me"), and I wouldn't
become part of the evil empire that is NYU if you paid me.
(NYU has single-handedly ruined most of the Village, including
the dog run in Washington Square: they built this huge building
that casts its shadow over the park, so that areas of the dog run
are perpetually in shade.)

Sometimes I get in these moods where everything I see or
think about depresses me. Everything seems like evidence that
the world is a shitty place and getting worse. I remembered feeling that way in Washington and attempting to put a positive
spin on all the things abandoned along the highway, and I tried
to do that on the train, but it was impossible, as we were passing through a particularly ugly (and depressing) section of the
Bronx.

Then we left the Bronx behind us and clattered across the
trestle bridge that connected Manhattan to the rest of the world,
and I could see it out the window—the glass towers reflecting
the morning sun, a sort of shimmering haze of heat just beginning to blur the sharp focus. And I told myself: Look at that,
look at New York, you love the city, it's your favorite place in the
world. But all I could think about was what was awaiting me
there: my mother, who would be furious I had disappeared again
after promising not to, and John. Every time I started to feel a little better and think that maybe things weren't so bad, I'd remember John telling me that I was a fucked-up kid, and picture him

sitting on the bench in the park, his head in his hands, moaning *There is nothing I want more than that*, and I would feel awful again.

I wished that Grand Central Terminal were a station and not a terminal, like Penn Station (although most people incorrectly refer to Grand Central as Grand Central Station), so the train would pass through and continue on to somewhere else, so that I could pass through and continue on to somewhere else, or just continue and never arrive, never stop. Spend the rest of my life in transit, safe inside a train, with the impossible unfortunate world hurtling past outside the windows.

Everything seemed very calm when I let myself into the apartment. In fact it appeared to be deserted. I stood in the living room for a moment, trying to discern if anyone was home. I wondered if they were out searching for me or at the police station. Then I heard the piercing wail of the coffee grinder in the kitchen, and walked down the hall. Gillian was standing at the counter in a T-shirt, grinding beans. The noise of the machine masked my entrance, so when she turned around and saw me she was shocked. "Christ!" she said. "Where did you come from? It's very creepy to do that."

"Are you making coffee?" I asked.

"No," Gillian said. "I'm doing a scientific experiment. Of course I'm making coffee. Are you an idiot?"

"Well, make some for me, please." I sat down at the table. "Where's Mom?"

"I don't know." She poured water into the coffeemaker and

turned it on. "In bed, I think. Or out, maybe. I just got up, and I'm in a very bad mood, so I wish you'd leave me alone."

"Why are you in a bad mood?"

She turned around and looked at me. "Why am I in a bad mood? I'm in a bad mood because people like you—in fact not *like* you, *but* you—ask me questions like 'Why are you in a bad mood?' after I've asked them to leave me alone." She returned her attention to the coffee.

I didn't say anything for a moment, and then I said, "You know, you're really turning into a very nasty person."

She didn't answer, just studied the coffeemaker, as if it were a scientific experiment. When it had finished brewing, she poured coffee into two mugs. She got milk out of the refrigerator and poured some into each cup and then added a spoonful of sugar to one. She brought the mugs over to the table and put the sweetened one in front of me. I was stunned: it was totally unlike Gillian to customize coffee (or anything) for me.

I sipped it and said, "Thank you. It's very good."

She didn't drink her coffee, she just held it in her hands as if they were cold and she needed to warm them. After a moment she said, "I'm sorry."

"It's okay," I said. "I'm used to it."

"No," she said, "you're right—I can really be very nasty. I'm awful."

"You're not awful," I said.

"Yes, I am. I'm awful. And I'm not going to argue with you about it."

"Fine," I said, "but I don't think you're awful."

Gillian didn't answer. She had a strange quivery look on her face, as if at any moment she might burst into tears. We drank our coffees in silence for a minute or two and then Gillian suddenly said, "I'm in a bad mood because Rainer Maria dumped me."

"He dumped you?" I asked. "What happened?"

"Yes," said Gillian. "His wife got some fantastic job running the universe at Berkeley and they've offered him a job, too, and so they're moving out there and turning over a new leaf and recommitting themselves to one another and reaffirming their vows and a lot of other stuff too revolting to mention."

"Well, that's not dumping you. He didn't dump you. He may be leaving you, but he isn't dumping you. There's a big difference."

"Yes, that's a point he tried to make, but I fail to see the difference. It's just a question of semantics. I suppose that's the price you pay for loving a language theoretician."

"Well, I'm sorry," I said. "I liked R.M. I'll miss him."

"So will I," said Gillian in an unnervingly unironic way.

"Well, maybe it's all for the best. I mean, he was a nice guy and everything, but he was married and a lot older than you. Maybe now you'll find someone more appropriate."

" 'Someone more appropriate': you sound like a guidance counselor, James. And you're hardly the one to give advice— what do you know about love?"

"Nothing," I said.

"My point exactly," said Gillian.

"I've changed my mind," I said. "You are awful."

This rapidly deteriorating conversation was fortunately halted by the sound of my mother coming down the hallway. Gillian said, "Don't say anything about this. She doesn't know."

"She doesn't know what?" my mother asked. She stood in the doorway, wearing a bathrobe, her hair disheveled from sleep. She seemed in a bit of a daze, but that's not unusual, as my mother often begins (and ends) her day in a daze. Neither of us answered her question and she apparently forgot she had asked it. She just stood there looking at us as if we were curiosities. Then she said, "James," and walked over and sort of patted me on the top of my head. Then she said, "Coffee," and walked over to the counter and poured herself a cup. Then she sat down at the table with us. I waited for her to continue her naming game and say "Table," or "Gillian," but she just sipped her coffee and looked vague.

I decided that given her stupor it was best to take the initiative. "I'm sorry," I said.

She looked at me. "You're sorry?"

"Yes," I said. "I'm sorry. I promise I won't do it again."

"I should hope you'll never do it again! And really, it's John you should apologize to, not me."

"I did apologize to John. But I'm not talking about that. I'm sorry about disappearing."

"Oh," she said. "You disappeared?"

"Yes," I said. "I didn't come home last night. You didn't even notice I was gone?"

"Ah—no," my mother said. "I didn't. I had a very unpleasant evening with Barry and was consequently a bit preoccupied."

"Not to mention a bit inebriated," said Gillian.

My mother glared at her, but apparently this hurt, for she winced and massaged her forehead.

"I can't believe you didn't notice I was missing," I said.

"Get a life, James," said Gillian. "You're eighteen years old. Do you still want Mommy to tuck you into bed?"

"No," I said. "I just thought someone might notice that I never came home."

"Oh, we would, eventually," said my mother. "You just have to stay away a bit longer next time. Where were you last night?"

"At Nanette's."

"I see," said my mother. "And how is she?"

"She's fine. Well, actually she seemed a bit tired. In fact she was taking a nap when I got there."

"You've got to be kidding," said my mother. "That woman wouldn't nap if you held a gun to her head."

"Well, she was. She was sound asleep."

"I don't believe it," said my mother. "She abhors napping. She thinks it's an indication of a weak character."

"Actually," I said, "it was her father who thought that."

"Her father? How do you know?"

"She told me," I said. "She told me all about him. He sounded like a tyrant."

"He was," said my mother. "Well, I suppose the apple doesn't fall very far from the tree. Like father, like daughter."

"Yes," I said. "And like mother, like daughter."

For a moment I could tell my mother didn't get what I

meant, and then she got it. She looked at me with a sort of hurt, amazed expression. "You think I'm a tyrant?"

"I think you have tendencies toward tyranny," I said. "And I wish you wouldn't say mean things about Nanette. She's my grandmother and I love her, so I wish you'd stop saying nasty things about her all the time."

Her amazed/hurt expression grew. It was like she was an actress and the director said, More, more, make it bigger!

"I'm sorry," I said. "I don't know why I said that."

She reached out and clasped my hand. "No," she said. "*I'm* sorry. James, I'm sorry. I'm so sorry. I won't ever do it again. I promise."

"Thank you," I said.

"This is all so touching," said Gillian. "It's like an after-school special."

My mother began to glare at her again but caught herself in time. She turned toward me. "Well, James, all I can say is if I had realized you were missing last night I would have been very upset and angry. You promised your father and I—no: your father and me—that you would never do that again."

"I know it's none of my business," said Gillian. "But it's almost noon. Shouldn't at least one of you be at the gallery?"

"I no longer work at the gallery," I said.

"You quit?"

"No, I was fired."

"By who?"

"Who do you think," I said. "Mom."

Gillian looked at my mother. "You fired James? Why?"

"I fired James for reasons that must remain confidential. But he has been reprieved."

"What?" I asked.

"You're no longer fired," my mother said. "John called me after you left yesterday afternoon. He had been thinking about things and felt he overreacted. He's still quite upset and angry about what happened, as am I, but apparently he feels able to continue working with you. Consider yourself very fortunate, James."

"What happened?" asked Gillian. "What did James do to John?"

"It's none of your business, Gillian. This is between John and James and me."

Gillian turned to me. "What did you do to John?"

"I sexually harassed John," I said. "Or at least that is what's being claimed."

"It's being claimed because it's true, James, and the sooner you understand that, the wiser you will be."

"What did you do to him?" Gillian asked me.

"I'm sorry," my mother said, "but I don't want to be a party to this conversation. I wish you'd talk about it elsewhere, some other time."

"That's ridiculous," said Gillian. "You're telling us what we can and cannot talk about in our own home?"

"Yes," said my mother. "That is exactly what I'm doing, but as you have never listened to me or done what I asked, I hardly expect for you to change now. Your characters are fully formed. My work here is done. I'm going to go take a shower."

The phone rang. Gillian answered it, and then she said, "Oh, hello, Jordan. How are you? Are you enjoying your time in the city? Oh, good. Did you? Really? That's so funny. I saw it Tuesday night. Amazing, yes. Isn't she incredible? Talk about chewing up the scenery—did you see her clawing at the walls? You're kidding—two nights in a row! How did you get tickets? No, he hasn't seen it, but I'm sure he'd love to. He's right here. Just a second."

She put her hand over the mouthpiece and turned to me. "It's Jordan," she said.

"Jordan?" I asked. "Jordan who?"

"Jordan, your roommate. I told you he called yesterday. He wants to talk to you." She held the phone toward me.

"Your roommate?" my mother said. "At Brown?"

"Yes," said Gillian. "Jordan Powell. Or Howell. He's charming. He called James yesterday and I told him James would call back last night, but I guess what with running away to Grandmother's house he didn't get around to it."

"I told you I wouldn't call him back," I said. "He's not my roommate. I'm not going to Brown."

"Please," said my mother, "don't start that nonsense again."

"It's not nonsense and I can't start it again because I never stopped it."

"One second, Jordan. James will be right with you," Gillian said. She walked around the table and held the phone out toward me. "James, don't be an asshole. He's called you twice. He's being friendly. He wants to take you to see *Long Day's Journey into Night*."

"Tonight?" I said.

"Yes," said Gillian. "He got up at five o'clock this morning to wait on the cancellation line. Talk to him." She thrust the phone at me like a gauntlet, but I didn't take it. My mother started to say something but stopped. They both looked at me, my mother imploringly and Gillian challengingly. And then Gillian did a strange thing. She said, "Please, James." She spoke softly, in a voice I had never heard her use, and then laid the phone very gently on the table in front of me. She returned to her seat.

A faint, faraway voice called out from the telephone. It said, "Hello? Hello?"

There was an odd hovering moment of stillness in the kitchen where time seemed to warp or stutter a little, and then the little voice called out again. This time it sounded disappointed, almost plaintive, as if it were afraid of being abandoned.

I didn't know what to do. What could I possibly say if I answered the phone? How could I talk with both Gillian and my mother sitting there, listening? But then I realized this terrible moment would go on forever unless I did something, and the only thing I could think of doing was to pick up the phone, and the only thing I could think of saying was "Hello."

17

October 2003

THERE'S A STRANGE MEMORY I HAVE OF MY GRANDMOTHER. I've never shared it with anyone, not even her, because it's kind of spooky and I'm not one hundred percent sure that it happened. It's one of my earliest memories. I must have been about four years old, maybe even younger. I was staying at my grandmother's house—I don't know why, or for how long, but I was with her and it was just the two of us. It was a sunny, warm day early in the fall, and my grandmother had spent the morning replacing the screens on her porch with panes of glass. And then, of course, she cleaned all the glass so it was sparkling, so that the porch caught and refracted the sun like a crystal. Anyway, because it was such a nice sunny day we were having lunch on the porch, sitting across from each other at the table that was pushed against the windows. I don't remember what we were eating, but I can remember sitting there, at the table—the table was painted red—and the bright square of sun coming through the glass and falling on the table, falling on me. And I remember my grand-mother said to me, Why don't you scooch over out of the sun, you won't be so hot. And I did, I moved down the bench out of the sun, to the part of the table that was in the shade, and continued to eat my lunch. I don't know how much time passed—it couldn't have been long because I was still eating whatever it was I was eating—when suddenly the glass window pane I had been sitting beneath fell out of its grooves and crashed down upon the table and the bench, right where I had been sitting. And it was clear it would have crashed down on me, on my head, had I still been sitting there. I remember we made light of it—we laughed and said it was a good thing I had moved out of the sun, and my grandmother swept up the shattered glass, and we finished our lunch. It wasn't until later, years later, when I remembered this incident, that it occurred to me that something strange had happened. Something miraculous. I don't know if the falling glass would have killed me—probably not—but I realized, in retrospect, that my grandmother had saved me, if not from death, then from terrible injury.

I'd always wanted to ask my grandmother about this memory. Does she remember it? Did it happen? Did it freak her out, or did she, like the child me, assume that love could naturally result in clairvoyance? But I'd never spoken to her about that memory. I think I was afraid that if I talked about it, if I let the memory be articulated, it might vanish, or decompose, the way some fragile and precious ancient things turn to dust if they are unearthed.

❖ ❖ ❖

I did go to Brown, and maybe it was leaving home, moving away, that made me resolve to finally ask my grandmother these questions. But she died on October 13, 2003, about six weeks after I left for school. It turned out that she had been having a series of small strokes—the first one probably occurred on the day I visited her, and found her uncharacteristically napping—but she didn't tell anyone, and she finally had a massive stroke. The mailman found her lying on the slate floor in the front hall. Apparently she had fallen down the stairs. So I will never know if this memory is real. But I think it must be, because I can remember it, and I don't think you remember things that didn't happen.

Because my grandmother didn't believe in funerals or burials or anything like that, there was nothing for me to come home for. I wanted to come home anyway, but my parents told me not to, that she would have wanted me to stay at school, for everything to go on as it had been. I think they really thought if I came home from Brown I might never go back, because I was miserable that first semester.

Her house is for sale, and sometimes when I'm online I go to realtor.com. I don't search for houses in the Midwest anymore. I look at my grandmother's house: *16 Wyncote Lane, Hartsdale: Charming Antique Tudor, All Original Features, Needs Modernization and TLC.* I take the virtual tour. It's like you're standing in the center of each room and turning slowly around, and you can turn around and around as many times as you like, the room continually spinning around you. The floors and the walls are like photographic negatives: squares of unfaded wallpaper where paintings once hung, the hardwood floors still burnished and brown where they were covered by rugs. The rooms are all empty, everything is gone: all that's left of her are these ghostly remnants.

She did leave everything in her house to me. My parents wanted me to sell it all to an "estate liquidator," someone who comes in and buys everything, and then liquidates it. That's the word they use: *liquidate*. But I refused. With some of the money my grandmother left me, I'm paying to have everything stored in a climate-controlled warehouse in Long Island City. I had them take everything, even the *National Geographic* magazines, the Castle at Heidelberg ceramic dish, the phonograph and all her records, including *The Fountains of Rome*. My parents thought I was crazy. Be reasonable, they said: Why pay good money to keep back issues of magazines in storage? Keep the things you may want, the things you could use, but sell the rest. Get rid of the junk. Liquidate it.

But it seems reasonable to me. I'm only eighteen. How do I know what I will want in my life? How do I know what things I will need?